FATAL PHANTASM

THE FATAL SERIES
BOOK 4

MAGGIE SHAYNE

OLIVERHEBERBOOKS

PUBLISHER'S NOTE: This is a work of fiction. Names, characters, places, and incidents either are the product of the author's imagination or are used fictitiously. Any resemblance to actual persons, living or dead, business establishments, events, or locales is entirely coincidental.

Published by Oliver-Heber Books

0 9 8 7 6 5 4 3 2 1

✿ Created with Vellum

CHAPTER 1

The most familiar eleven notes of Chopin's *Funeral March* droned from the programmable doorbell's hidden speakers. Kiley probably should have taken that as a sign.

She was snuggling with Jack on the sofa, watching their favorite TV show, and making fun of the phony ghost hunters' manufactured fear of static sounds on their digital recorders.

She wasn't sure how life could be as good as it currently was, but it was damn near perfect. Their ghost busting business was providing the whole gang a steady income, the house was amazing, Lady El was minding her own beeswax (mostly,) and she and Jack were damn near perfect.

Hush, sister. You wanna jinx it?

The house ghost's face superimposed itself over the TV show, translucent, like a reflection. Tonight, Lady El wore a gold turban, her lashes were a jungle, and her jowls were a little bit saggy.

"Someone's at the door," Jack said.

"Yeah, I guessed that by the doorbell. And who added the Funeral March to the repertoire?"

That was me. Lady El, puffed her cigarette, and blew lavender-scented and non-carcinogenic (she promised) smoke at her. Kiley was usually the only one who could smell it, or even see her, which was weird, her being a full-on muggle and Jack being sort of a ghost-whisperer.

Just had a feeling it was called for, Lady El said, or thought or whatever. She didn't speak aloud, but inside Kiley's head. Or something.

"So are we going to get the door?" Jack asked.

"Nope." Kiley snuggled closer. "It's the business entrance, and business hours are over."

The ominous notes played once more.

"They aren't taking no for an answer, though." Jack self-extracted from the snuggle.

Kiley grumbled but got up, taking her phone with her, as one does, and followed him deeper into the house, past the staircase, to the room that used to be a library and now served as Spook Central HQ. Yes, it was a ridiculous name. But it had been used by the best. Buffy, the Ghostbusters, even the Scoobs. The original ones.

"Maybe we should get a dog," she said to Jack as she stood beside him at the French doors. A female shape was on the other side of the semi-sheer curtains she'd put up because it was creepy sitting in front of bare glass on a dark night in a place spooks loved. "Better not be another damn ghost. Then again who else would show up at this ungodly hour?" She glanced in passing at the antique mantel clock she'd found in the attic, but it had stopped at 1:13, possibly days ago at 1:13.

Lady El looked back at her from the glass that covered the clock's face. A copper red curl hung out of her shimmering gold turban, resting artfully across her forehead. *It's called an eight-day clock because that's how often you have to wind it, Einstein.*

Kiley ignored her, and tapped the phone in her hand. 8:38. "Who knocks on a door at 8:38?"

Sister, you're older than me, and I'm dead!

Jack opened the doors.

The woman who stood on the other side had masses of thick blond hair spilling down past her shoulders and wore a clingy dress with a neckline so low and a hemline so high they nearly met. She reeked of money.

Kiley hated her on sight, and Lady El hissed like a cat or a vampire or something.

The woman at the door flashed a toothpaste commercial smile, breathed Jack's name, and then she hugged him.

She fucking *hugged* him.

Kiley cleared her throat. Loudly.

The blonde released him, and he had the good sense to back up until he was standing right beside Kiley. He even took her hand, which made her smugly confident. But he didn't say anything, and he seemed shocked or worried. He kept looking at her, and then at the woman, and then at her, and then at the woman.

Rolling her eyes, the blonde reached past him and stuck out a hand. "You must be Kiley," she said. "It's good to finally meet you."

Kiley took the bait, so she had a grip on her hand when she went on. "I'm Julie, Jack's ex."

"Ex-what?" Kiley didn't mean to crush her hand, but she must have because *Julie* winced and twisted it free.

"Wife," she said. She rubbed her hand, then lowered it to her side, and smiled brightly.

"Oh." It came out like a squeak. Kiley cleared her throat, squared up and said, "Oh, *that* Julie." Because she'd be damned before she would admit that he hadn't told her. Ex-wife? Ex-*wife*? What the actual—?

Told you not to jinx it.

Kiley looked up at Jack. His eyes were round, guilty, and

maybe pleading. Hers were probably like barbecue skewers stabbing into them. There was a dangerous burn behind them, though, and while she didn't much care to leave them alone together, she thought it best she get the hell out of there before she did something that couldn't be undone and would result in prison time.

"I was just, uh, heading upstairs," she said with all the dignity she could muster in her jammies and furry penguin slippers. And then she pivoted and left the office. She even closed the double doors behind her.

Are you out of your mind? Leave the doors open ...unless you're going to listen outside it ...wait you're still walking. Why are you going upstairs?

Kiley didn't reply to her pesky but lovable ghost and continued to her room. She closed the bedroom door behind her, blinking her hot eyes. She would not cry. She would not cry. She would not cry.

Don't cry! Spy! Lady El stood in the mirror. It was a big one, so Kiley could see more of her. She wore a white dress that hugged her substantial curves from boob to ankle, its skirt ruched to hell and gone. Her belt, necklace, and earrings were all gold, like the turban. *You should be listening in.*

"I'm not that insecure." She was, though. Sure, she'd been badly burned by the guy before Jack. The one who'd romanced her just long enough to get her account numbers, and then stolen her entire inheritance, which had been substantial. She'd convinced herself it was unfair to carry that baggage into her relationship with Jack. She was completely over that. She'd left it behind.

Those tears tell a different story, sis.

"Yeah, so does the feeling of my heart being crushed all over again." She knuckled her eyes dry. "But it's just anger. Besides, I trust Jack."

Seriously? You trust him? Still?

El made a good point. If Jack would keep a secret this big from her, what else might he not have told her? Hell, she didn't even know he'd been a shrink until it had come up in a case. And the suspicious monster she'd put to bed was waking up and it was pissed.

But she would not reduce herself to acting like a jealous, insecure lover. If you didn't trust someone the solution wasn't to spy on them, it was to dump them.

Oh, hell. That was *not* a fun thought.

Fine. If you won't spy, I will. El puffed her cig, blew the smoke into a big cloud that covered her reflection entirely, and vanished from behind it.

Kiley paced. She talked to herself. She swore a lot. She told herself this wasn't the same. It wasn't at all the same. Mark—if that had even been his real name—was nothing like Jack. Jack was a good man, she knew he was.

Oh, God, but she'd thought his predecessor was too, once.

She took off her penguin slippers and threw them at the wall. And then she heard Jack coming up the stairs. Must've been a short conversation.

It was, and there was no further touching, either. Oh, she reached for his shoulder, but he turned away—pretty elegantly, too. I don't like her, though. Not one bit.

"Thanks, El."

Jack opened the bedroom door and stood there like he wasn't sure whether to come in. She faced him from four feet away, composing an intelligent and unemotional question in her mind. What came out was,

"What the actual fuck, Jack?"

He lowered his eyes. "It was ...we were in college. It only lasted six months."

"You were married."

"Yeah."

"And you didn't tell me."

"I was going to tell you, but then it felt like I'd waited too long, and then ..." He trailed off.

So he didn't have a reason. Hell, she'd hoped he might have some perfectly logical, valid reason. "This is a big deal," she said. "First, I didn't know you were a shrink. Now, I don't know you were married to a freaking Kardashian? What's next?" Her eyes widened. "Do you have kids?"

"No. Look, Kiley, she means nothing to me. It's been fifteen years. I haven't even seen her since—"

"You are missing the point by light years, Jack." She closed her eyes. "I trusted you."

His eyes took on a wounded look. "Past tense?"

"Well, once someone lies to you, you'd have to be an idiot–"

"I never lied to you."

"You lied by omission, and you know it." She lowered her head. "Maybe ...you should go."

Go? What do you mean, go? Lady El shouted so loudly in her head that Kiley found it hard to believe Jack couldn't hear her. Hell, she was surprised the whole neighborhood couldn't hear her. *Just give him back to her, why don't you?*

Ignoring Lady El, she tried to meet Jack's eyes, but that just made hers swim with more tears. "I've been lied to before. You know that."

"I know," he said. "But I'm not a con out to steal you blind, Kiley. I'm your ...your guy. I love you."

He's the best thing to happen to this house in centuries, sister. And the best thing that ever *happened to you. And you know it, oh yeah, you do.*

"Will you just shut up!"

"I guess that's fair," Jack said. "You need some space. I can ... go bunk with Johnny for a couple of nights."

It's. A. Big. House. Dumbass.

Kiley closed her eyes, took a deep breath, tried to feel her own feelings. She didn't want him to go. She wanted him to make it okay again.

"It's a big house," she said, even though it would feed El's ego. "I can have space with you here."

Thank you, sweet Jesus. In the mirror, Lady El fanned herself with the most elaborate fan Kiley had ever seen. It had huge, fluffy white feathers and gold sparkles.

"Speaking of space ..."

All right, all right, I can take a hint. I'm gone.

"You're right," Jack said. "I'll go."

"I didn't mean you." Kiley reached out for his arm because he'd started to turn away. "It was El."

"Look, I don't know what you want. You want me to go? You want me to stay? Just tell me what you want. Don't make me guess, cause I stink at it. You know that about me by now."

He looked at her, waiting, and she opened her mouth, closed it again, and then decided that since their relationship was crumbling before her eyes, she might as well be honest. "I want you to have told me about her from the beginning. I want this never to have happened. And short of that, I don't fucking know what I want."

"I was going to tell you. I've been planning to tell you, and then things happened, and I didn't. And then it seemed better just to ..." He turned his palms up. "I'm an idiot. And I'm sorry."

"I know you are."

"Wait, which one?"

"Both. But you were *married*. Jeeze, Jack, you lived with that woman. You slept with that woman every night. You snuggled on a couch and watched TV with her. You shared a home and bills and meals and—"

"It wasn't like that. But I know this is a lot. And thank you for the offer to let me stay, but I think I'd better give you some space. This all happened pretty fast, between us. It wasn't what you had in mind."

"Wasn't what you had in mind, either."

He pressed his lips tight and came closer, took both her hands and said, "For what it's worth, I get why you're mad. I don't blame you. I'm aware I screwed up, and I'm sorry."

Ohhh, that's good. You gotta admit, that was good.

She shrugged. It was a start. It wasn't everything she wanted to hear.

Well, sure! You want him to say you're better. Prettier, kinder, more fun to be with, better in bed, and that he's way happier with you than he ever was with her and that— El popped into a mirror, one hand on her chest, the other arm out wide — *and that he knew not what love was until he set eyes on you.*

Kiley rolled her eyes.

Lord, why can't I talk to him instead of her? Lady El asked the ceiling.

"I love you," he said. Then he kissed her forehead.

She didn't respond in kind. She just walked past him out of the room, headed downstairs, and went to the kitchen to make a cup of something soothing. Wine, she decided.

Do you know what he's doing up there?

Kiley jumped so hard the wine she'd just poured sloshed onto her chin before she even got the first sip.

Packing. He's packing!

"It's fine. He's right. This isn't something you just breeze past. It's serious."

You wanna talk about serious? I am dead. *This is a tempest in a teapot. A bump on a log. Teats on a boar hog. It's meaningless. You don't want to be alone.*

"Tonight, my friend. I really do."

She refilled her glass and carried it back to the staircase, because Jack was coming down, a little black satchel in one hand. It was reassuringly small.

He met her eyes and gave an awkward smile that broke her heart a little. She walked with him through the little foyer to the front door. He said, "I'm only a few minutes away if you need me."

"I know."

"Okay."

"You um ...never said what she wanted. Probably none of my business but—"

"She's being haunted, wants to hire us. That's as far as she got. I told her it was a bad time. She's supposed to come back tomorrow during business hours. Ten a.m."

"You can't possibly think we're taking the job."

He shrugged one shoulder. "I thought we could hear her out and discuss it. Isn't that what we do?"

Wrong answer. You are blowing it, Jack! Lady El shouted even though she knew Jack couldn't hear her.

Kiley lowered her head, didn't answer.

He hesitated a second and then he just left. Just opened the door and walked out.

"He didn't kiss me goodbye," she whispered as he got into his stupid van.

Damn, Lady El said. *I'm gonna miss watching that man shower.*

CHAPTER 2

Johnny texted her, and in spite of all Maya's efforts, her heart jumped for joy when his image lit up her screen. She loved the look on his face in that shot she'd assigned to his contact info, three-quarter profile, chin low, eyes looking up at the camera, wearing the kind of smile that made you wonder what he was up to.

But then she read the message.

"Jack just showed up with baggage. Maybe check on Kiley."

"On it," she texted back. And then she stared at the screen for a full minute, watching for those promising ellipses dots to appear. They didn't. Johnny had bought her fake relationship with Joe, hook, line, and sinker. And that was what she'd wanted. It was why she'd asked Joe to play this stupid game to begin with, so Johnny would let go of his hopeless romantic ideas about the two of them and fall for somebody else. Somebody younger, closer to his own age.

She was doing the right thing by him. It was the right thing.

Sighing, she thumbed her phone and texted Kiley, who had somehow become her very best friend. She didn't even have to think about what to say. She typed it fast.

"I need a venting & vodka night. U in?"

The dots appeared, because girlfriends didn't leave each other hanging. "Can we do it here? In jammies?"

"Obvi. B there in 20." Maya got off the sofa, where she'd been watching Hallmark movies and debating the pint of Ben & Jerry's Cherry Garcia in the fridge. She wouldn't even have to change clothes. Her nightgown could double as a sundress, and her silk kimono would make the perfect bathrobe.

She grabbed her slippers off the Turkish rug on the hardwood floor. Her modern, asymmetrical house had been under construction for two years, and she was finally in it and was in love. She had a studio now, soundproof for making videos and podcasts and recording audio versions of her books about Witchcraft and natural magic.

It was everything she'd ever dreamed of as she'd built her career. She'd mastered the internet early on, and become one of its reigning stars, at least in topics of the occult and things that go bump in the night. She'd poured heart and soul into her online persona, and it was paying off beautifully. But somewhere along the way, she'd forgotten to look for a partner. And she was finding that success wasn't worth much without someone to share it all with.

She closed her eyes to imagine her someday man, but Johnny was right there in her head, not taking no for an answer.

Dammit.

She ran upstairs to pack a change of clothes, a toothbrush, and shower supplies into an overnight bag. Then she raided her gourmet-worthy kitchen, tossing in every comfort-snack she could think of, and adding the Ben & Jerry's for good measure. She grabbed a bottle from the liquor cabinet behind the wet bar and headed to her car with a backpack over one shoulder and a canvas grocery bag in her hand.

She hopped into her spanking new Tesla and sat there a

second, looking back at her place. It was a beauty, sided in sustainable bamboo stained to enhance the grain. One side of the green shingled roof was steeper than the other. The back had a two-story window that looked right out onto the stream that flowed through the woods.

She'd done really well for herself. She ought to be happy.

So why was there this yawning hole in her chest where her heart was supposed to be?

Her phone buzzed. She gave it a glimpse as she got into the car. Joe Fantone's goofy mug looked back at her. She rolled her eyes, hit the speaker button, and said, "Why don't you text like the rest of the world?" as she backed out of her driveway.

"Why don't you answer your phone with 'hello' like the rest of the world?" he asked.

"What do you want, Joe? I'm in the middle of something."

He sighed. "I wanted to touch base about the barbecue."

Right, the barbecue. They were supposed to be cooking out and painting Kiley's house all next weekend. She'd planned to cap the day off with a kick-ass summer solstice enchantment to keep malevolent spirits at bay. Now she wondered if the painting party would even happen.

"What about the barbecue?" She reminded herself she wasn't mad at Joe. Joe was her friend, and he was only doing what she'd asked him to do. It wasn't his fault she was miserable. She wasn't entirely sure what was up with her crappy mood, but she knew it wasn't Joe's fault.

"I think we should postpone staging our breakup until after the party."

"Why?"

She could almost see him taking off his glasses and polishing them as he talked. "A breakup right before the party would be a bummer. And they need all the hands they can get, and I *am* pretty handy with a paintbrush."

She sent the speaker a look and got out of her own head long enough to see through him. "Aw, you want to go to the party, don't you?"

He sighed. "Yeah. I admit it, I do. It's just ...since we've been fake dating, I've started to feel like part of the gang. And after we fake break up, that's probably going to end, and I'll go back to being an ordinary high school science teacher again, without a ghost-busting side gig."

She took the left onto Kiley's street and thought Joe wouldn't be out of the gang if little Breia had anything to say about it. She flirted with Joe openly—right in front of her sometimes.

"Okay, that's cool. We can break up after the party. And I don't think you're going to be ousted from the gang when we do. If you want to keep hanging around, keep hanging around."

"I don't know. Is um ...everything okay? You sound weird."

Joe knew her pretty well. Maybe too well. But what was she going to say? *When the phone rang, I hoped it would be Johnny.* That would be insulting even to a fake boyfriend.

"I'm fine. And it's sweet of you to ask."

"We're friends. Not many formerly-dating-currently-fake-dating-people can say that."

She laughed. "You think?"

"So should we meet up beforehand so we arrive together, or ...?"

"It's a week away, Joe. Can we decide later?"

"Okay. All right. Sorry, you know my penchant for planning ahead."

"I do, yes." Joe was the most organized guy she knew. He was like a walking life-planner.

"All right," he said again. "You have a good night then."

"Bye, Joe. Talk to you soon." She disconnected, pulled into Kiley's driveway, and piled out of the car, bags and all, and when she got to the door, she tried to make it open just with her will, but it didn't budge.

She'd slammed it that one time, when they were under attack. But hadn't been able to repeat the trick since. No telekinesis at all.

She pressed the doorbell with her elbow. It chimed the opening notes of Chopin's *Funeral March.*

Kiley opened the door. Her eyes were puffy, and her cheeks had red tear tracks, and all Maya's selfish concerns evaporated. "Aw, hell, girl, what did he *do*?" She crossed the threshold, dropped the bags and went in for the hug.

"Not much." Kiley's words were muffled by Maya's shoulder. "Just forgot to tell me he was married."

Maya stepped back, wide-eyed. "Jack is *married*?"

"*Was* married. To a freaking centerfold."

"To a—"

"Not a real one. But she qualifies." Kiley bent to pick up the grocery bag, and Maya followed her through the living room and dining room to the kitchen at the back of the house, dropping her backpack at the foot of the gorgeous hardwood staircase as she passed.

In the kitchen, Kiley unloaded the bag's contents onto the counter; chips, dip, a huge bag of chocolate bars, two bottles of wine, one of vodka. Two pints of ice cream...

She sent Maya a questioning glance. "This is all vegan?"

"You won't even notice."

"Sure I won't. That's what all you vegans say. And I do notice."

Maya turned to the cupboard for a pair of glasses and set them on the counter. "So, tell me what happened."

Kiley shook her head. "It was such a good night. I was thinking how good things were. Yes, Lady El, you told me not to jinx it." She rolled her eyes and re-started. "So there we are, all cozy on the sofa and the doorbell rings, and it's this bombshell. *Julie.*" She said the name as if its vowels tasted sour her tongue. "She has this ass, and these boobs, and this tiny little waist, and this hair tumbling all over the place, and I *know* that was filler in her lips. Nobody's lips are that thick. And she hugs him! Just throws her arms around his neck and hugs him! Right in front of me."

Maya started to open the wine, but Kiley shook a hand at her, then twisted the cap off the vodka. Then she looked at the toaster and said "Damn straight," to, Maya guessed, Lady El. She'd give her eyeteeth to be able to see the late jazz singer herself, but she only appeared to Kiley. At least so far.

Kiley poured way too much into her glass. "Leave room for ice and soda," she said, taking the glass with her to the fridge to add both. She returned with the soda and a handful of ice for her own glass.

"Hi, I'm *Julie*," Kiley said, dripping sarcasm. "I'm Jack's ex-wife, *myeah myeah myeah.*" She tipped the glass back.

"You didn't start without me, did you?" Maya already knew she had.

"Only a little."

"You're gonna be sick tomorrow."

"Maybe I'll die." Then she grinned at the toaster. "Lady El says it's the best thing she ever did. Ha!"

Oh boy, Maya thought. It was going to be a helluva night.

SOME TIME LATER—WHO knew who much?—the doorbell played the Funeral March. Again. Kiley lifted her head, opened her eyes, but the room and her head swam, and she dropped it back again. "Maya," she said, and the sound of her voice hurt her head.

"What?" Maya's reply was a moan in the shape of a word.

"The doorbell's broken."

"Sounds fine to me," she said, but the words were muffled because her face was still pressed into a sofa pillow.

Kiley peered at her friend through squinty eyes. Maya had apparently made a bed on the floor from some chair cushions. The chairs stood around naked. A pizza box was on the floor beside her. The writing scrawled across the inside of its lid said, "Brian, 555-1234. Call me." Kiley wondered who Brian had been hoping would call, her or Maya? Maybe both.

"Keeps playing the same dire shit," she said finally, "but it's set to shuffle."

It played again as if to provide an audio-illustration of her words.

Maya pushed herself up in the hungover version of a modified cobra pose, and said, "Well, *that* can't be good."

The door creaked open, and Jack's cautious "Kiley?" was followed by an alarmed, "*Kiley!*" He came running inside, put his hands on her shoulders and shook her. It was probably only a little, but it felt like a 9.2 on the Richter scale. Leaning closer to her face, he said, "Are you okay? What happened?"

"Sssstop mmmoving me," she said, and he immediately backed away, averting his face from her brewery breath. "I'm fine." Kiley sat up, pulling the sofa throw she'd used for a blanket with her, then took a surreptitious look to be sure she was clothed. Yep, same jammies as yesterday, only wrinkled and bearing splotches of pizza sauce.

"I'm fine, too," Maya said. "Not that anyone asked."

Lady El laughed at the comment, but Kiley was the only one who could hear her.

Jack was looking around the room. No doubt, it was a mess. Lady El's old record player was on in the middle of the carpet, surrounded by albums, one of which was still on the turntable.

The needle was brushing the record's innermost groove over and over.

And where did that mutilated pile of jelly donuts come from?

"We have a meeting," Jack said. "Did you forget?"

"That's not til ten."

"It's nine forty-five."

Kiley put her feet on the floor and reached for her phone. Her reflection in the screen startled her so much she jumped a little. Her hair looked like a tangle of briars and deadfall that had been electrocuted.

"Bring *Julie* in the business entrance when she arrives," she said with way more confidence than she felt and a heaping scoop of sarcasm on top of the name, which seemed to be the only way she could say it. "We'll be there right on time."

She glanced past him, because the rest of the gang were arriving. Joe and Chris came in first, followed by Johnny and Breia who were in an animated discussion when they entered. That caught Kiley's attention. There was something going on between those two. It didn't feel like a romance any more than Maya's relationship with Joe did. But there was something.

Her brain replayed a snip of the night before; off key laughter, a "fuck men" toast, the taste of straight vodka, followed by a sloppy confession from Maya. "And fuck faking it with Joe just so Johnny will move on."

The vision swam in and out of Kiley's mind, and her eyes locked with Maya's and she could've sworn her bender-buddy knew exactly what she was recalling.

Johnny was heading for Maya, looking all worried, but she held up a hand to stop him. Their eyes met, and Kiley didn't know how everyone in the room couldn't see how bad they wanted each other.

Preach! Lady El said way too loudly inside Kiley's brain.

She got off the couch, took Maya's hand, pulled her to her feet, and then right up the stairs. Without slowing her pace, she called, "Make some coffee for your wife—I mean, our new client, Jack."

"What?" That was Breia.

Kiley held Maya's hand all the way to the top of the stairs, then they split, Maya heading into the guest room she always used when she slept over. She'd had the good sense to bring an overnight bag, and she'd thrown it in there early on in their evening.

Kiley went into her and Jack's room. The bed was still made. She hadn't slept in there. Not just because she'd drowned her sorrows all night in the living room, but because it just wouldn't feel right, climbing into their bed alone.

She showered fast, dried her hair, and brushed her teeth twice. When she spit out the last mouthful of suds and lifted her head, Lady El stood behind her in the mirror and she jumped, a hand to her chest. "Jeeze, can you not sneak up on me like that?"

Telling a ghost not to sneak is like telling a bird not to fly. It's how I move.

"Oh, come on, you could make some noise."

El shrugged and took a thoughtful puff from her smoke in its long holder. Today she wore blue sequins on a low-cut, tight-fitting gown. Her wild red curls spilled out from all sides of a sparkling headband that looked like it was encrusted in real diamonds.

Of course they're real diamonds. Why would I conjure myself fakes?

"What do you mean, conjure?"

Conjure. Create. Imagine into existence.

"You can do that when you're dead?"

You can do it when you're alive, too, sister. The living just don't remember how.

"Huh." She pulled on some ankle length skinny jeans, a brown cami with lace at the neck, and a cute short jacket, like a thin Bolero, unbuttoned. Then she opened the closet and stood considering her choice of sandals.

So is showing up late a power play or are you just being rude?

"*She's* being rude by being here at all."

There was a tap on the bedroom door. "She just pulled in," Maya called from the other side. "And she's not *that* hot."

"Only a best friend would lie like that." Kiley shoved her feet into a random pair of shoes, then opened the bedroom door. "I've applied minimal makeup and Visine. How am I?"

Maya looked her up and down and gave a nod, so Kiley returned the favor. Their resident witch had pulled her still damp angel hair around to one side in a long, fat braid, and like Kiley, had slapped on some makeup. She looked good. Maya always looked good. She was as ageless as a Norse Goddess. Hell, she deserved a young stud like Johnny.

"You look good," Kiley said.

"I've got your back," Maya replied.

When they walked downstairs, they moved as one, shoulder to shoulder. The smell of strong coffee met them halfway, and they both closed their eyes in pleasure and made the same "mmmm" sound. Just the aroma was helping Kiley's headache, or maybe the handful of Ibuprofen she'd swallowed. Either way...

The aroma got stronger as they neared the bottom, because Jack was waiting there with a steaming mug in each hand. He passed one to Kiley and said, "I'm really sorry. Really, *really* sorry."

She met his eyes and had the immediate, dual reaction of wanting to kiss his face and wanting to smack it, but settled for taking the coffee and a grateful sip. Then she closed her eyes and breathed, "Thanks," before thinking better of it, then had to look past him to avoid eye-contact. The living room had been restored to order.

Then she was looking at Jack again and cursing herself for looking at Jack again. His half-smile was the saddest thing she'd ever seen. Her heart felt sore and achy as she went down the hall toward the big double doors. Behind her, Maya said, "Nice move, Jack, but you're gonna have to do better than coffee. I think a grand gesture is in order here. And by grand, I mean, major. *Huge*."

Nice to have a girlfriend, isn't it? Lady El said, her eyes gleaming up from the shiny antique doorknobs.

"Yeah. Who'd have thought?" Kiley lifted her chin and pushed the doors open, breezing into Spook Central headquarters like she owned the place. Because she did. Breia, their resident dark-haired pixie and former client, was on the far side of the room keying information into the computer. Johnny had campaigned to get her hired after the latest uptick in cases. Summer was changing to fall, peak season for the ghost-hunting biz and their new house-clearing service had become so popular they could barely keep up.

Johnny's eyes were all over Maya, openly concerned. He rose from one of the cafe-style chairs when she came in.

And then there was *Julie*. Perched on the edge of the sofa so *somebody* would have to sit beside her.

Rawr! Lady El said.

Kiley marched across the room right to her, plopped her ass on the sofa right beside her, put both hands over hers on her skinny thighs, met her eyes, and said, "I'm so sorry about last night. Thanks for understanding," aloud and *Stay the fuck off my lawn* silently.

"It's fine. I understand needing to set boundaries between business and personal time."

"I'm very big on boundaries." Kiley reclaimed her coffee mug from the table in front of them and scootched closer. No way was her man sitting beside *Julie*. "This is Maya Rand—"

"I know." The ex rose from the sofa, extending a hand Maya's way. Maya had to take three steps closer to shake. "I've seen your videos."

"So has everybody," Kiley said, and told Maya with her eyes, *Don't you dare fall for her flattery*. "Obviously you've met everyone else. So why don't you tell us why you're here?"

"It's um...my husband. He died recently."

Which means she's single and on the prowl, Lady El observed. Everyone blurted some form of "Sorry for your loss," which Julie acknowledged with a nod before going on. "There's some jewelry missing. Pieces that are precious to me."

"Jewelry" Kiley repeated.

Julie tilted her head to one side like a model who knew her angles. "I've been reading about you in the papers. It seems like you're for real."

Real as a heart attack, lady, El muttered.

"And you think your dead husband knows where this missing jewelry is?" Johnny sounded as skeptical as Kiley felt.

"I have no idea." She raised her palms with a little shrug and too many blinks. You know, like would be cute if she were sixteen. "But I thought maybe you guys could do whatever mojo-jojo you do," she wiggled her fingers when she said it, like a cartoon character casting a spell, "and talk to him, or contact him so I can talk to him, to find out where it is."

"That's it?" Kiley asked.

"That's it," she replied, and she got to her feet.

"We, um, don't have much luck talking to those who've crossed over," Jack said. "It's really the ones who are stuck here—"

"Well, that's the thing," his ex said a quickly. "I think ...I think he is. Stuck, that is. In our beach house. That's where we spent our last several months, as his health declined too much to travel. It was his favorite place. And it's where he died. I think if you can reach him at all, you'll be able reach him there." She rummaged in her designer bag and pulled out a little business card with an address on it. And then she withdrew another card, a postcard sized, laminated obituary card with her grandpa's photo on it. No. It was her husband's.

Kiley passed it to Johnny, who passed it on, then went back to the business card, which had nothing but an address on it. No, not an address. A name and some coordinates.

"Where is this? Wanderer's Keep? What is that?"

"Our private island. It's on a barrier island off the North Carolina coast. I'd like you to come for the weekend. All of you," she said.

Oh wouldn't she just love to get Jack out there on her private island for the weekend where she can work her wiles on him. I do not think so. Lady El sounded good and pissed.

"If you can find the jewelry, I'll pay you fifty thousand dollars."

Well, Lady El said, *maybe we should consider it.*

CHAPTER 3

Maya choked on her coffee.

Jack said, "We'll have to discuss––"

And Kiley blurted, "Sold. Breia, print up a contract with our standard rates plus a fifty-K bonus when we find it." Then to Julie. "We'll deduct our rate from the fifty if we find the jewelry. But we're getting paid, even if we don't. That work for you?"

"Kiley, I don't think—"

"I know you don't," she said, cutting Jack off, and it was kind of mean, but she was kind of pissed.

"Done," Julie said.

Breia started tapping keys. She'd become useful, helpful, and she saved them more money than they paid her because she was an amazing bookkeeper. Even her kid brother Ryan helped out sometimes after school. But that wasn't why Johnny had pushed for Breia's hiring. Kiley didn't know the real why. Not yet, anyway.

As for Joe, he sort of hung around and did his best to help. He was unpaid labor and so far, not good for much as far as ghost busting was concerned, but he knew science and he was smart. Maybe a genius, but Kiley didn't know that for sure. He sure seemed like a genius, though.

"We'll discuss your case and call you after we decide," Maya said. "That's how we do things."

Kiley looked at her bestie sideways, chin low, eyebrows high.

Maya looked straight back at her, unflinching, even adding a nod.

Julie took her cue and headed for the French doors, but as she went through them, she sagged to one side, like her knees had gone weak, and caught herself on the doorframe when Jack didn't run over there to offer assistance as she had no doubt intended. Then she headed out around the house via its gorgeous sidewalk.

The gang had cleared the weeds and debris away to reveal a flagstone path that went all the way around to the driveway. They'd used some of their profits to have their broken sign replaced. Chris and Johnny had installed it together. It stood out front, near the driveway, and it had an arrow pointing toward the business entrance. The sidewalk and sign had eliminated the problem of clients showing up at the front door and having to traipse through the residence to the office.

Boundaries, Kiley had discovered, were the key to using her home as their business headquarters. And really, where else would they put it? The place had ambience, and ghosts seemed to love it.

When Julie's car revved, the gang's tense silence broke. Chris said, "What is she driving?" and ran to the window to catch a glimpse as she backed out. "Porsche. *Nice.*"

"I thought you had my back," Kiley said, speaking to Maya as if nobody else was there.

"I do, hon, but you can't just say yes to a client without discussion. You might not be objective about this."

"Maya's right," Johnny said. "We always discuss a case

privately before deciding whether to take it." He used that soothing tone that he used when he spoke to dying souls who were afraid to cross over, very deep and soft, but steady and strong. Come to think of it, the last three of those cases he'd worked on, he'd taken Breia with him. Interesting, Kiley thought. What was up with that?

She snapped out of it in time to realize everyone in the room was nodding in agreement with what he'd said.

"We have a policy," Maya said. "We all voted on it. We meet the client, hear their case, discuss it, and vote. Yes, no, or further research needed."

"We all agreed," Jack said. "You agreed, too."

They've got you, toots. Lady El appeared in a diagonal slant of sunlight on the window glass.

Kiley lowered her head.

"It's understandable you're upset," Maya said. "I'd be furious too if an ex-wife I knew nothing about came crawling out of my man's past." She shifted a glance Jack's way as she said it.

"I heard that wife comment before, but I thought maybe you were still drunk," Briea said, sliding off the stool at the computer bar. "So Julie is Jack's ex-wife?"

"And you didn't know?" Chris asked, also rising. He was their resident computer nerd and, until Joe came in, the smartest member of the gang.

Jack looked around at all of them, raised his hands palms up. "I know, I know. I'm guilty. I'm an asshole. I messed up. But I was a college kid and it only lasted six months and it feels like a different lifetime and ..." Then he shifted his focus to Kiley. "Why the hell am I having this conversation with anyone but you?"

"You're right, Jack." Johnny delivered a compassionate shoulder pat. "This is private stuff. We don't need to know."

"*I* need to know," Chris said. Briea elbowed him.

Kiley closed her eyes, took a breath, opened them and found Jack gazing at her, all pathetic and please forgive me. Damn him.

"Let's move the subject off my love life and onto the matter at hand," Kiley said. "The question before us is whether to talk to a ghost, help him cross over, and find some missing jewelry for the widow Kendall, or turn up our noses at an easy fifty-k. Discuss."

Maya said, "I think it's going to cause unnecessary strife between you and Jack."

"Issues about me and Jack need to be off the table," Kiley said. "Let's keep our focus on the business."

"Okay then, I think it's going to cause unnecessary strife between partners in this business." Maya crossed her arms and gave a little huff that blew her hair off her forehead.

Johnny was looking at her when she did so, and he almost smiled, just barely caught it in time. Why didn't they realize they adored each other?

And the sea accuses the sky of being blue.

"What the hell kind of cryptic bullshit is that?" Oh, crap, she said that out loud. "Not you guys. Lady El."

"What did she say?" Jack asked.

"Talk to your own ghosts, Jack. I've only got the one."

The working theory was that Kiley's powerful connection to the house was the reason she was the only one who could see the late jazz singer, Eleonore Petrenko, aka Lady El, who upon her death in 1969, had bound her spirit to the place she'd loved best.

"Anyone else have input here?" Kiley asked.

Breia said, "I don't think she's telling us the whole truth."

Everyone looked at her and Kiley was relieved there was a new topic. "What made you think that, Breia?" Kiley asked.

She shrugged.

Johnny said, "Maybe we table the decision for now and do a little background research?"

"Wait, I want to hear Brie's answer. What are you basing that on?" Kiley pressed.

Breia closed her eyes for a second. Kiley thought she might be replaying the conversation in her mind, so she could tell her which of Julie's actions or expressions or turns of phrase had made her suspect dishonesty.

Wouldn't it be great if she turned out to be a lying sack of—

Breia opened her eyes. "I don't know. I just felt like there was something more." She shrugged. "But I'm just a muggle."

That was the phrase that felt less than honest to Kiley, and something about it niggled at her brain.

"Where are you getting this, Bray?" Kiley flashed Johnny her palm when he started to speak. "You've been different ever since you died that day in the living room."

"Who wouldn't be?" Johnny blurted.

But there was a look between the two of them that spoke volumes. Kiley saw it, and she saw Maya see it, and then they looked at each other.

"I agree with Johnny and Breia," Chris said. "Let's do a little digging first. Then we can decide."

"Think how we could spend that fifty grand," Kiley said. "We could have the place professionally painted. We could fill every bookshelf in here with rare books on the afterlife. We could get an official company vehicle."

"I think we should vote," Johnny said. He was getting pretty damned cocky now that he wasn't the newest member anymore. "All in favor of taking the case immediately?"

"Aye!" Kiley said it as if volume counted.

"One in favor," Johnny said. "All opposed to taking the case at all?"

"Nay!" Jack and Maya sang out in perfect harmony.

"Two opposed," Johnny said. "All in favor of tabling a decision pending further investigation?" He raised his hand as he said it, his "aye," low and polite. Chris and Breia did likewise. And so did Joe, who didn't really have a vote, but voted all the same. "That's four."

"Who the hell had the idea to make this thing a democracy?"

"You did!" Everyone said at once.

Jack lowered his head so she couldn't see his eyes.

They broke like an NFL huddle and headed off to gather further info on Julie Kendall, agreeing to reconvene in at seven.

MAYA WAS deep into her research when her doorbell rang. She went to the window and looked out to see Johnny's pickup in the driveway, and immediately headed to the closest mirror to check herself over. Like a teenager with a crush. God, she was pathetic.

She was in jeans and a pretty white cotton blouse with a tough of lace at the collar and hemline. Nothing fancy, just lounge-around-the-house stuff.

She ran down the short stairway to the entry, and opened the door wide. He smiled at her and held up a bag of tortilla chips. "You have guac?"

"I always have guac."

He grinned. "I knew that. And I was craving some. Plus, I thought you might want a hand with the research."

It only took one hand to move a mouse around a mousepad, but she wasn't going to call him on that. Johnny clearly had something on his mind, and besides, she wasn't quite selfless enough to resist spending time with him. He was the person whose company she enjoyed most, after all.

She held the door and he came inside, heeled off his shoes and they went up the stairs together, into her living room. It was the biggest room in the house, and she loved it's tall windows and their views of the sky and the trees and the little stream in back.

"I'm set up over on the sofa," she said, nodding that way. He followed her gaze to her open laptop. "I'll get the guac. And some salsa. And ...something to drink? I have iced tea, coffee, or wine."

"Ice tea sounds great," he said.

"You sure?" She asked. "It's unsweetened–"

"WIth a little lemon. I know. That's how I like it."

"Me, too."

She hurried into the kitchen-dining room combo. It was an open floor plan, so she was able to glance his way repeatedly— more accurately, she was unable to *not* glance his way repeatedly —as she poured two tall glasses of iced tea from the pitcher she always kept in the fridge and carried them back. Then she returned for the container of guacamole she'd just made day before yesterday, a jar of store-bought pineapple salsa, and a big bowl for the chips.

Johnny poured them in when she set the bowl on her coffee table, and immediately attacked the container of green dip. After crunching for a couple of seconds, he said, "You make the best guac."

"Yes I do. So you gonna tell me why you're really here?"

He smiled at her. "Not to hit on you, promise. I got the memo. But I thought ...I don't know, you seemed a little off and I wanted to check in."

"Oh, that."

"Yeah, that." He sipped his tea while Maya thought of reasons she could give him for being "a little off" that were not the real reason. The real reason was that her ridiculous attraction to him was not going away as she'd expected it would once they stopped sort of dating. So what else might be bothering her?

"I'm worried about Jack and Kiley." It was the best thing she could come up with on short notice.

"Yeah, so am I. But I don't know what Kiley's worried about. Jack is completely into her. He doesn't have any interest at all in Julie. Guys can tell these things about each other."

"Oh, can you now?" She said it with a teasing lilt.

"Oh, we can," he teased right back.

"Well, I think she knows that. It's not that she's worried he might prefer Julie, it's that he kept the marriage a secret from her."

Johnny mulled on that a moment while crunching down another guac-coated chip. "I can see that, I guess." The he shrugged. "I wonder why he didn't tell her?"

"I can't even imagine. I think they'll work it out, though. Don't you?"

"I do," he said. He leaned back on the sofa and sipped his cold tea. "I'm glad that's all it is. I was afraid it might be something else."

Should she ask, or should she leave that alone? Oh, hell, she cousin't resist. "Something specific or—"

"Yeah. Breia and Joe."

She blinked at him and he quickly held up a stop sign hand. "Not that there's anything going on between them. I'm sure there's not, it's just the way she acts sometimes with him. It's gotta be kind of infuriating."

She studied his face. His brown eyes were like melted chocolate to her. Just as appealing, just as irresistible. And his face, and his hair, oh, god, his hair, like long black silk she wanted to run her fingers through over and over and—

She took a gulp of her tea to try to derail that train of thought. "It does irritate me, to be honest. But I don't know. I don't think Breia's doing it on purpose."

"No, I don't either. I do think Joe ought to shut it down, though. You know, gently."

Yeah, he really should. If he was really her boyfriend and not just pretending to be.

"She's such a delicate thing, though," she found herself saying. "He's just being careful not to crush her, you know?"

He nodded. "I can talk to Breia about this, if you want. I don't want to overstep, but I think she'd listen to me. She and I have become pretty close."

"Yeah, I've *noticed*." She said it before she could stop herself, and the words carried a distinct aroma of jealousy. "I mean ..."

"We're just friends. You know that, right?"

She shrugged one shoulder and gazed at the computer screen, where her social media search results on Julie Kendall were stacked to the moon. "I know. Sure I know. I mean, it's none of my business anyway."

He was looking at her oddly, so she clicked a search result, and a video of Julie Kendall striding down a runway in a charity fashion show with local celebrity models. When she pivoted to go back, she fell off her high heels and landed in a graceless heap. The video cut off just as the emcee bent to help her up.

"Man, the comments are brutal," she said, skimming the cesspool section.

"The comments are always brutal. It's how cowards get their kicks, insulting others anonymously. I hate the comments section."

"I do, too."

He met her eyes. "You get that shit, too."

It wasn't a question. "It comes with the territory. And I'm expected to not only reply to every comment, but do so without calling the writer an ignorant, barely literate asshole."

"Must be all but impossible," he said. "I could never exercise that kind of self-control."

"Sure you could, Johnny. You just close your eyes, take a deep breath—"

"And count to ten?"

"And call down the wrath of Hecate on their ignorant, barely-literate asses."

He laughed softly.

"Seriously, though, I have a couple of fans who jump all over them. And while I have to put out those kinds of fires before they blow up my social, I have to say it does make me feel better."

"Good. I'll keep at it then."

She blinked at him. "You ...you aren't ..."

"Spiritualguy365," he said, tapping the brim of an invisible hat, "at your service."

His smile made his eyes crinkle at the corners, and they sparkled into hers, and she could barely keep herself from leaning closer and kissing him.

His phone chirped, and the spell was broken. He broke eye contact to check it and said, "Jack says he needs my help with something. I should probably go."

"Yeah," she said. "Okay. Um ...thanks for stopping by, Johnny. And for caring that I seemed off and for shooting down nasty commenters."

"Any time," he said, and then he headed out.

She followed him to the door, but it wasn't necessary. He stepped into his shoes and gave a nod and left. Maya closed the door behind him, turned and leaned back against it. "Girl, you have to get over this shit. He's too young."

CHRIS BROUGHT PIZZAS, including a vegan one for Maya, and they broke their own rules and ate in the office, though Kiley had insisted on plates and had a jumbo roll of paper towels on hand.

They were all gathered around the computer bar along the back wall, Chris manning one, Breia at another. Breia was wearing a cute sun dress with big purple and yellow pansies and a green cardigan she swam in. She had a file open to take notes. On another computer, Chris was running the show.

Johnny stood right behind Chris's chair, Maya on his right, and Joe on her right, which happened to be directly behind Breia's chair. Kiley and Jack were the bookends. It was symbolic of how she felt about their relationship right now. They were way too far apart.

"This is Wanderer's Keep," Chris said, and tapped play on a video he'd set to full screen. And it was a huge screen.

The camera panned over clear blue waters and tropical looking woodlands. She realized it was drone footage as the view swept over the long slender finger of island. One end rose high above the Atlantic, with steep rocky cliffs. Along one side of the island, a few small houses lined the shoreline. As far from them as possible, on the opposite end, a white sand beach stretched out to the sea. There was a short pier with a few boats attached. There was a boathouse too.

"Julie Kendall was born in Texas but left to attend Cornell University," Maya said, having scanned the net for background info.

"You went to Cornell?" Kiley asked, shooting Jack a look that should have set his hair on fire.

"Yes, for a frat party. Yet another deep dark secret I've been keeping."

"Oh, that's good, Jack. Act like *I'm* the bad guy."

Not in front of the children, Lady El advised. *Did you find a gold compact in that box of my treasures from the attic?*

He sighed, lowered his head and asked, "Did she graduate? I never knew."

Kiley rolled her eyes, but he didn't have the sense of self-preservation to shut up.

"Yes," Maya said. "It doesn't even mention that you two were married anywhere I could find on the web, other than the state's public records. The annulment is in there, too." She cleared her throat and shifted a sideways look at Kiley.

Interesting. Annulment, not divorce. Also, what about that compact?

"I haven't seen your damn compact."

Maya leaned forward to look around Joe at her. "Lady El?" And when Kiley nodded, "I think I saw a compact when we were rummaging in the attic. Gold-plated?"

Plated my ass!

Kiley was still too angry to smile. More angry than Jack having been married before probably warranted, and more than even his not telling her about it deserved. It was that he'd damaged her trust in him. It had been hard for her to let herself believe in him, having been so wrong about the last guy she'd believed in. It hurt being so blindsided ...again.

Ohhhhh. Well, that explains a lot.

She rolled her eyes, and nodded at Maya to get on with it. Maya was reading from her phone.

"Her first job out of college was at *Wealth Magazine* and six months later she was promoted to editor and married to its media magnate owner, Arthur Kendall."

The drone footage on Chris's computer was showing the grounds now. There were gardens complete with water features in the back, a tennis court, an elaborate pool with a natural looking stone waterfall, and a twisty dirt track that led down among those cliffs.

Then the house came into view, and Kiley almost choked. It was a Mediterranean-style mansion the size of a hotel, and a connected series of crystal-clear pools reached to its steps on one side.

"Just so you know," Chris said. "I don't fly. I don't care if it's paradise or not, I just don't. You all decide to go down there, I'd just as soon stay here and hold down the fort."

"Ryan could help you out," Breia said, offering up her kid brother.

"Wouldn't he want to go?" Chris asked. "Free weekend in paradise and all that?"

"Yeah, no. He doesn't ever want to be anywhere near another ghost.But he could help out around here."

"At Spook Central?" Chris asked.

"Of course. When our enraged late parents went ballistic on us, this was the only place where they couldn't get to him. It was his haven. This house saved him."

She means I saved him, Lady El said.

Kiley said, "You and the house are pretty much the same thing, El. You're this place's soul."

"Literally," Maya added, even though she hadn't heard Lady El's side of the conversation. Then she went on, returning to her phone notes. "Julie Kendall is on the board of several charitable organizations, and there are rumors she's been quietly running the magazine for the last several months as her husband's health declined. Rumor has it her own health hasn't been great, either, but she denies that any time she's asked." She glanced Kiley's way. "Maybe she's not that bad."

"Maybe she really needs our help," Joe said softly.

"Even though I don't think she's being completely honest with us, I think I agree with Joe," Breia said.

"Big surprise there." Maya said it under her breath, but everybody heard.

Breia frowned as if she was puzzled and Johnny averted his face so nobody could see what he was feeling.

Kiley spoke quickly to cover for her. "Are we really going to turn down a weekend in freaking paradise and getting paid to be there? I mean, come on guys. I can handle being around Jack's ex for that long.

I really need that compact, Lady El said.

"Yeah, but can *he*?" Johnny asked, looking Jack's way with sympathy.

Jack sighed. "We were going to paint the house this weekend." He twisted his mouth to one side, then lowered his head, and asked, "Anybody need anything from the kitchen?" Then he headed for the door. But he looked back at Kiley to ask with his eyes to come along.

"I guess we're discussing this alone. In the kitchen," she said.

But my compact ...

The stream of cussing Kiley uttered was not pretty, but when she ran out of words, she sent a sweet smile Maya's way and said, "Will you please retrieve that compact before I decide to *call an exorcist!*" She cranked up the sarcasm as well as the volume on those final three words.

"We *are* exorcists," Breia said.

"Well, sort of," Joe put in, and they shared a goofy grin, and Maya looked at them like she wanted to knock their heads together.

Kiley left the library behind Jack and trailed him into the kitchen, where he turned around without a word of warning, pulled her into his arms, and kissed her like the end of *Romancing the Stone*.

When he came up for air, he said, "I love you. Only you. I fucked up. I'm sorry. Can we let this thing go?"

"It's not that I don't want to let it go. I'm trying to let it go. But you hurt me," she said. "You know how hard it is for me to trust.

And I trusted you, like really, totally trusted you. And you deceived me."

"I didn't see it as deceiving you, babe, I swear. I wanted to tell you, intended to tell you, and I'm *going* to tell you everything from now on, I swear to God. I'm already making a mental list of things from my past to tell you about. I'll tell you so much you'll get bored and beg me to stop."

She lowered her head, closed her eyes. "I love you, too. You know that, right?"

"It's nice to have it re-confirmed," he said. But the way his body went from uncooked noodle to cooked noodle told her he'd been worried it wasn't the case. And he cared.

He came in for the hug, but she sidled away.

"My heart is bruised and my trust in you took a severe hit."

"I know. I'm so sorry."

She nodded. "I believe that."

"Good."

"I still want to take the case."

"I know you do." He opened the fridge, took out a gallon jug of apple cider, and set it on the table. Then he went for glasses. "What I don't know is why." He had five glasses, three in one hand and two in the other. "Last night, you didn't even want to take this meeting."

Kiley picked up the cider jug. "We should make her wait until February. It's miserable here in February."

As they headed out of the kitchen, he said, "Tell me why you really want to do this."

She shrugged. "I don't know."

"Honesty goes both ways, though," he said, and he said it kind of softly, like he was tiptoeing over a land mine.

"I mean it. I really don't know," she said. "Maybe part of me needs to see you with her, just to be sure. Or maybe part of me needs to know her better, so I can figure out what it was about her that made you fall in love with her."

"Alcohol made me fall into bed with her. Love was never a part of it. She got pregnant. She wanted to keep the child, and was going to drop out of Cornell, where she had a full scholarship, to raise it. So I offered to marry her, take care of the baby so she could finish school. It was not a romance. It wasn't even an attraction, it was a couple of stupid, drunk kids at a frat party. And that's all it was."

They'd made it all the way to the staircase that spilled into the living room and the hallway around behind it that led deeper into the house, but Kiley stopped walking. "So you got married. And ...and there's a child?"

"We went to a justice of the peace. We didn't even move out of our dorms. We were going to figure out our living arrangements later, when the baby came. She miscarried before it ever got that far."

"You didn't even live together?"

He shook his head side to side.

"But you stayed married for six months, you said."

"It took six months to get the annulment. And to be honest, we didn't break up for several weeks after the miscarriage. It was a loss, you know. We helped each other through it. We liked each other. We even became friends, but it was pretty apparent that the pregnancy was the only reason we were together, and that reason had ended. A judge agreed, and annulled the marriage."

She nodded slowly. "Thank you for telling me all that."

He tried a half smile, and there was a lot of relief in it, but it evaporated when she added, "But I still want to take the case."

CHAPTER 4

Six first-class tickets to the gorgeous Carolina coast were waiting for them at the airport. Joe had selflessly volunteered to sub in for Chris. *Julie* had flown back on her private jet right after the meeting. She'd offered to send it back for them on Friday, but Maya had objected so strongly on environmental grounds that they'd opted to fly commercial. First class was a happy substitution. And it was a short flight, really.

A limo picked them up at the airport and drove them to a pier, and under an hour later, they were in deck chairs sipping cocktails as their vessel carried them out into the Atlantic.

Well, Maya and Kiley were in deck chairs. Johnny and Jack were leaning over the rail on one side. Joe sat by himself, basking in the sun. Breia had yet to sit still, she was so excited. She ran from one side to the other, looking and pointing and shouting. "Look at those birds. Look at that fish. Look! Dolphins!"

"Is this a yacht, do you think?" Kiley asked.

Maya lifted her brows. "I don't know. I do okay, but I'm not yacht-rich."

"I think it's a yacht."

The table between them was affixed to the floor, or deck, or whatever. Their pilot, Kevin, wore white shorts and a white shirt with gold braided blue shoulder patches that would probably get him beaten up by anyone who was really in the Navy. He even had the hat.

Julie had probably insisted on it.

He was all teeth and tan. He'd given a brief welcome aboard speech, asked what they'd like to drink and then vanished, only to return with all of their orders on a tray like the best of cocktail waitresses. Then he promptly delivered each drink to the wrong person.

They smiled at each other as he walked away presumably to drive the boat, then they exchanged beverages and resumed basking.

Maybe the Kendalls weren't rich enough to afford a bartender *and* a yacht pilot.

Maya sipped her screwdriver, which she'd ordered with a "Why not? We're spending the weekend in paradise."

Johnny and Jack each had a beer in a frosted glass mug.

Joe asked for wine and Breia had a cola.

"Chris and Ryan don't know what they're missing," Joe was saying.

Breia said, "Paradise or not, I feel better that he's at home with Chris. Besides a private island isn't a seventeen-year-old's idea of a good time. He'd rather have wall-to-wall gaming computers and an endless supply of McDonald's meals."

Kiley sipped her vodka-diet on ice, and watched the coast shrink smaller and smaller behind them. And then still smaller, and then it started to kind of fade into nothingness. "Hey, how far out did she say this place was?"

"Five miles?" Maya said. Then, more softly, "So, are you and Jack okay?"

Kiley glanced at her man, standing there talking quietly with Johnny, watching the ocean skim by far below. He was still the best looking man she'd ever seen, and she still got that delicious tingle whenever their eyes met. "I think we will be. I took a hit, you know? I'm still sore and punch-drunk."

"I get that. But he didn't keep staying at Johnny's. That must be a good sign."

"And how do you know he's not staying at Johnny's?"

"Don't wiggle your eyebrows at me, woman, you know I'm with Joe."

"I know the exact opposite," Kiley said, and nodded at the glass in Maya's hand. "Liquor has a way of bringing out your secrets."

"Shit. The other night?"

Kiley nodded. "Don't worry, I won't tell. But"—she leaned closer—"what I don't get is why Breia's flirting with Joe pisses you off so much if you're not really with him."

"Because she doesn't know that."

"Oh."

"I mean as far as she knows, she's hitting on my man under my nose," Maya said.

"Oh."

"Women shouldn't do that to each other."

Kiley tilted her head toward her left shoulder, then her right shoulder. "Is that what she's doing, though?"

"What do you mean?"

"I mean, isn't there a chance she senses that you and Joe aren't for real?"

Maya's eyes widened and her brows rose. "I never thought of that. You really think she's onto our little ruse?"

"I don't know. She's been different since she died that time. There's something up with her."

"I agree," Maya sad. "And I think Johnny knows what."

"Johnny only has eyes for you, Maya. He's freaking love-struck. And I think you should go for it."

Maya sipped her drink, and looked at Johnny's back across the deck. Kiley looked too. He and Jack were standing near the rail, looking out at the ocean.

"Oh, before I forget again—" Maya rummaged in the yellow straw bag she'd hung over the side of her chair and pulled out an elaborate compact shaped just like a clamshell, if clamshells were made of gold. "I found it, and then I kept forgetting to give it to you."

"Ohmygosh, you took it out of the house? El's probably having a breakdown about now." She took the compact from Maya. "Wow, that's heavy."

"Real gold, maybe?" Maya said. "I'm so sorry I forgot it was in my bag. I'll make it up to her. But ...you know it doesn't make much sense, her asking us to find it for her. It was right in the attic. She has full access to the whole place."

"That is odd, isn't it?" She turned the thing over, running her hands over it in case there was some message or symbol on it. Obviously, El had reasons for wanting her to have this thing in hand, and it wouldn't be the first magical tool the Lady'd had stashed in her attic. She'd had a penchant for the occult and used to hold seances in the house when she'd lived there.

"I'll make it up to her, though," Maya went on. "I'll... Oh! I'll do a podcast about her career, play some of her hits, even. You think that would do it?"

"All I know is that even *Julie Kendall* doesn't have a solid gold compact like this." Kiley was aware that every time she said the other woman's name, she loaded it with sarcasm, and she didn't care to correct it. She opened the compact.

Lady El smiled at her from its mirror and gave a dainty finger wave. Kiley squeaked in alarm and snapped it closed.

"What?" Maya asked.

"Um, I think Lady El *wanted* you to forget this thing was in your bag." Then she opened it again, slowly this time.

Lady El gave her a wide-eyed WTF look. *Well, that was rude.*

"Sorry. You startled me."

Isn't this great! I get to go on vacation with you!

"It ...sure is." Kiley nodded too much with the words. "So that's why you wanted the compact?"

Mm-hmm. I was able to travel using it once before. I think it has to do with its connection to the house. I found it there when I moved in, so ...

"What's she saying?" Maya asked. "Am I in trouble?"

"She *wanted* you to bring it," Kiley said. "You're off the hook."

The hell she is. I still want that podcast!

Kiley smiled. "But she still wants to be the subject of a podcast."

"Done," Maya said.

Wonderful! Lady El smiled so much her eyes crinkled at the corners. Then she took on a more serious expression and asked, *So, what's a podcast?*

THERE WAS a long pier extending from the island, with a couple of boats attached. A small boathouse with its huge doors flung wide sat a few yards farther along the shore. Their tanning-and-toothpaste model pilot assisted them off by way of a short gang-plank. They carried their own bags, but only as far as the pair of ATVs waiting on the shore. No drivers were provided, but Kevin helped load their baggage into the roomy cargo spaces on the back of each one. Johnny, Maya, and Joe were in one. Breia squeezed in with Jack and Kiley who slid over to give her a third of the seat. She did not take up all of it.

"This is really amazing, isn't it? I wonder how far to the house?"

Jack was driving them over a road. "A couple of miles, according to Cap'n Kevin." Jack said the name the same way Kiley usually said Julie's—dripping with sarcasm. Was he jealous, maybe? "We just stay on the main path," Jack said.

"It's gorgeous, I'll give her that." The road was a well-worn dirt track, and it meandered through a forest with so many different kinds of trees, it had to have been manmade.

"I wonder where the other roads go," Breia said. She craned her neck to try to see down every fork and turnoff, and there were several. "How big is this island, anyway?"

Joe said, "Maybe you can pull up that drone footage Chris found and see if you can tell from above."

"Great idea!" Breia pulled out her phone and tapped, and then tapped again, and then said, "Huh. No signal."

Jack and Kiley pulled out their phones the way a foot kicks out when its knee is tapped with a doctor's mallet.

"No bars," Jack said.

Kiley tapped her phone repeatedly, not believing her eyes. "All the money in the world and not a single bar. What the actual—"

"We'll probably be able to pick up wi-fi at the house," Breia said. She finally sat back down in her sliver of seat, tucked her phone back into her pocket, and looked at Kiley with a bright smile. She was as cute as was humanly possible, with her pixie short haircut, velvet brown eyes, and footlong lashes. But it was her nose that did you in. Kiley would've killed for a nose like that.

There wasn't a mean bone in her body. "Hey Breia," she asked, just to test her theory. "What do you think about Maya and Joe?"

"I love them," she said, emphasis on love. "Why?"

"I mean, about their relationship?"

"What're you doin', babe?" Jack said, *sotto voce, near her ear.*

"Oh, that?" Breia waved a hand and went "Pssssh. That's not real."

"It's not?"

"No way." And then, jumping as if startled, she said, "Oh no! Oh no!" And then her eyes rolled back in her head and she tipped sideways, right out of the ATV.

Kiley grabbed her by the blouse, but it tore and she lost her grip. Breia landed hard on the road, rolled once, and just lay there with road dust all over her light blue sundress.

Jack skidded the ATV to a stop, and behind them, Johnny stopped his, too. Everyone piled off and gathered around her.

"She's unconscious! Did she hit her head or something?" Maya asked, crouching low and checking Breia's head.

"I don't think so," Kiley said. "She passed out *before* she fell. And I think she knew it was coming." Kiley patted her cheek. "Breia. Breia, come on, wake up now."

"It's okay," Johnny said. "She's okay. She'll be back in a few minutes."

Kiley turned and looked up at him. Everyone else was kneeling near Breia, but Johnny was standing by and not sufficiently terror-stricken. Joe looked like he was going to pass out, too. He was pacing three steps then turning and pacing three in the other direction, while tapping numbers on his phone. 911 no doubt. "She's unconscious, Johnny. That's not what I'd call okay."

"No, it really is. Um ...it happens sometimes. And I will explain it to you later, but right now, we should get her someplace safe."

"Safe." Joe said it oddly. "What do you mean, safe?"

"Just ...you know, a nice soft bed and some privacy."

Maya straightened up to her feet. "And some privacy for us too, so you can explain what the hell is going on with Breia."

"She should be the one to do that." Johnny bent as if to gather her up, but Joe beat him to the scoop, lifting Breia easily.

"I've got her," Joe said. "Let's do what Johnny says. He obviously knows more about this than any of us."

For a man of few words, he'd said a lot. And there was a heap of something on top of it. Jealousy? Resentment? Toward Johnny?

Kiley wondered if maybe Breia's obvious crush on Joe was a two-way street, after all.

Joe carried Breia to the golf cart he'd been in and got into the passenger seat, arranging her carefully across his lap.

Johnny ran back to jump behind the wheel.

So Jack and Kiley mounted up and resumed the drive, with Maya squished into Breia's former seat.

When they rounded a curve and the place came into view, Kiley almost forgot about poor Breia. A series of pools gleamed crystal blue, right up to the wide stone steps of the mansion. The pools were divided by patios, walkways, and waterfalls. There were columns all along the front of the mansion's wide veranda and huge arched entry doors.

"This isn't somebody's house," Kiley said. "This is a resort. Nobody lives like this in real life." She looked sideways at Maya. "Do they?"

"Sure, some people do."

"She sure did trade up," Jack said. Then he looked at Kiley, his eyes all expectant.

Oh, right, she was supposed to counter that remark. "I got the better deal there," she said, and he looked relieved. Then she added, "Her man is dead, and took his secrets with him. Mine's alive, so there's still a chance I might hear them. Eventually."

He frowned. "You think Arthur Kendal had secrets when he died?"

Kiley nodded. "I'm with Breia on that. I don't think it's just some random missing jewelry she needs us to find."

Jack pulled around the only way an ATV could pull around, along a narrow, paved circle that bordered the pools and ended at a set of stairs that led up to the veranda from the side.

Johnny pulled to a stop beside him. Julie came into sight up at the top of those stairs, wearing a flowy, colorful kaftan and big white sunglasses. She waved at them as two young men in white shorts and matching polo shirts moved past her and went straight to hauling their bags off the ATVs and into the house.

Joe climbed out of the little all-terrain vehicle with Breia in his arms, limp as a Regency Miss with the vapors, and Julie's smile died.

"What's happened?"

"She has a ...a condition," Johnny said.

Joe nodded as if in agreement. "If we can just get her into her bed—"

"Of course. Jerry, take these two right up. Not the corner suite, that's for Jack and ...um ..."

"Kiley," Jack said.

"She knew that," Kiley muttered. Then she pulled out her gold compact and snapped it open as if that was a perfectly reasonable thing to do.

Fuck that bitch, Lady El said. *And might you figure out a way to leave me open, so I can see what's going on?*

Joe was led upstairs behind all their bags, but Julie was holding court in the foyer, which was two stories high and had a concave cupola at the top that housed a crystal chandelier. The room was so big it echoed. Terra cotta tiles lined the floors and walls in every swirly curly pattern you could imagine. There were gigantic palms and ferns and other potted plants around the place, arranged in front of windows that were twice as tall as a grown man. Everything was light colored, cream, tan, beige, palest brown. The accent pieces were green, the plants, area rugs, throw pillows on pristine white furniture. There were two staircases that bowed outward and led to the second floor.

"This place is amazing," Maya said, looking around.

"I'll give you the grand tour later. But I'm sure you'd like to get settled in first. Dinner is in two hours, if that's long enough?"

They all looked at each other, and everyone nodded.

"Okay, then follow me." She turned and went up the left staircase, and the gang followed her up like school kids in a fire drill. Kiley was trying to take in as much as she could of the place on the way. God, she hoped Breia was okay.

At the top of the stairs, Julie led them left and into a hallway. "All your rooms are in this wing. Maya, you're here, first room on the right. Your friend Briea is right next door, and then the corner suite is for Jack and Kiley since there are two of you." She pointed as she said it. "Johnny is across the hall from Maya, Joe is across from Breia.

"Do we need keys or something?" Kiley asked.

"It's not a hotel," Julie said. "The rooms are unlocked. Um, dinner will be poolside in two hours. Take your time and come out when you're ready. That's soon enough to talk business." She sent a worried look Jack's way. "Are you sure the girl is all right?"

"She is," Johnny answered instead.

"Okay, well, let me know if you need anything. Just pick up the phone in your room and it'll ring through to me."

They all kind of stood outside their respective doors, pretending they were about to go in, until she was out of sight, and then they all turned and stampeded into Breia's room.

She was lying in the bed, the covers pulled over her. Joe was standing beside the bed, watching her. As they all spilled in, he shot an impatient look their way.

"All right, Johnny," Kiley said. "Spill."

Johnny held up his hands and closed the door softly behind him. He took a breath, and said, "Okay, so, remember that time when Breia died and then came back?"

CHAPTER 5

"So whenever someone dies," Joe said, summing the long and complicated tale Johnny had just told the gang, "Breia astrally projects to their side to escort them into the ethereal plain." He spoke slowly, as if he was turning the idea over in his brilliant mind.

Maya knew that look of his. He was trying to figure it out. How it worked, what it meant, and probably the quantum angle of it all.

Kiley, who could always be counted on to put things more simply, said, "So Breia's the Grim Reaper."

"Not exactly," Jack corrected. "This only happens if the dearly departed is stuck somehow, right Johnny?"

Johnny nodded.

Maya was still trying to puzzle it out herself, even while trying to ignore the relief of knowing that *this* was the big secret between Johnny and Breia that she and Kiley had been wondering about. "So anytime someone dies and has trouble finding their way through the Veil Between the Worlds, Breia's soul leaves her body to help them find the way."

"Right," Johnny said.

"Well, that sounds like some kind of ..." She looked at the girl in the bed. Her sable, pixie-short hair stuck up like the feathers of an angry chicken. Something warm filled her chest. "It sounds like she's some kind of angel."

"I think it's something in between. Definitely not grim, and not a reaper. But not a full-on angel, either," Johnny said. "At least not most of the time."

Jack was pacing back and forth near the foot of Breia's bed. "She just gets sucked out of her body involuntarily? Without any warning? Without even her consent?"

"That's how it seems so far," Johnny said. "But it's only happened a handful of times. Even she isn't sure how it all works. Personally, I think she must have some level of control over it. She just hasn't figured out how to use it yet."

"What are you basing that on, Johnny?" Maya asked. Because she knew he wouldn't just spout theories without a basis.

"My grandfather. He told me nothing that happens to us is truly without our consent. There's no assertion, he said. Only allowing. It's a matter of finding your inner power and learning to wield it."

"I don't know about that," Joe said.

He couldn't help himself, Maya knew that. He believed in science. His brain must be getting a real workout now that he was an unofficial member of the gang.

"But this phenomenon," Joe went on, "has been recurring only since the day her heart and respirations stopped, and she was resuscitated." He studied Breia, rubbing his chin and nodding slowly. "That has to be what instigated the onset, then."

"She was between the worlds." Maya was kind of feeling her way to a theory, unlike Joe, who was trying to think his way to one. "She helped her parents cross over. Then she came back, and retained that ability somehow."

Kiley frowned at Johnny. "Why are you the only one who knows about this?"

He looked at each of them, and there was guilt in his eyes. "I hated keeping it from you guys. You gotta know that. But it wasn't my secret to tell." His gaze lingered longest on Maya's, and she knew he'd probably been dying to share this with her, get her thoughts on it. She knew that because, if it had been her, she'd have been dying to share it with him. That was just how they were with each other, even though they'd decided—she'd decided—they shouldn't date.

"Breia showed up in my living room that night."

"Right after her parents' second funeral."

"The one after we exorcised them," Kiley said.

"Right. She arrived in my living room, without her body. And she didn't know why she was there, or how. She thought it must have had something to do with me, but it wasn't. When I went to drive her home, we came upon the scene of an accident near my house," he said. "It was an old man. He'd died in his car. I don't know if the accident killed him, or if he died first and that caused the accident. But he was alone, confused and scared, just sticking close to his body, too afraid to leave it behind.

"And she helped him?" Maya asked in a reverent whisper.

"As soon as she saw him, she knew what to do. And yeah, she helped him. It was beautiful, just ...sacred, you know?"

"Wow." The word came from multiple lips.

"Well, why didn't she feel she could tell us?" Kiley asked.

Johnny shrugged. "She's been through a lot. It's a big change. I think she'd have told you guys pretty soon. She's barely had time to adjust to the idea herself."

Kiley nodded slowly. "Okay. I get that." Then she lifted her head sharply. "So *that's* why you were so eager to bring her into the business."

"Yeah," Johnny said as if it should be obvious. "I mean,

sending the dead to the other side where they belong is kind of what we do. It almost seemed like she was meant to be with us. Besides, she was scared and alone just like the people she helps —aside from her kid brother, and she sure wasn't going to dump that on his teenage shoulders after what they'd both just been through. She needs us."

"She needs us," Maya said. "And Breia and Ryan were led to us for a reason, I feel it right to my toes. Saving them from their disembodied parents was only the first part of it. This ...this is huge."

Everyone nodded or muttered in agreement. But Maya had returned her attention to young woman in the bed, and felt a ripple of unease dance up her spine. "How long does it usually take her to come back, Johnny?" she asked, taking hold of Breia's hand.

Johnny's dark brown eyes shifted to Breia, lying in the bed. It wasn't like sleep, the state of her body. It was more like death. Which scared the hell out of Maya. Was her hand cooler than it had been before? Wait, was her heart even beating? She felt around her wrist for a pulse, trying not to be obvious about it. Kiley saw, though, and caught her eyes, widening hers slightly. Maya felt a soft beat, though, and nodded once on a relieved exhale.

"It doesn't usually take very long," Johnny said. "She's there in a flash, even though she still sort of ...she still has form, even outside her body."

"She's not invisible?" Jack asked. "She can be seen by anyone?"

"Well, I can see her. And the dead can see her." Johnny shrugged. "I don't know about anyone else. I don't know if she knows that, either. Like I said, this is all new."

Maya saw the little crease forming between Johnny's

eyebrows. It reminded her sharply of his grandfather, and then she couldn't get the old man out of her mind.

He'd vanished, nobody knew where, but he'd managed to let Johnny know he was okay, and that he would see him again. Everyone was trying to find him. That was the case they worked on before, during, and after everything else. But John Redhawk had gone off the grid, and Maya didn't think he would be found until he was ready to be found.

Her attention snapped back to the grandson when Johnny said, "She should be back by now."

"Well, maybe she can't find her body," Kiley said. "I mean, when she left it, we were back on the road."

Joe went to the windows and yanked the heavy drapes wide, letting sunlight flood the room. Then he opened the window, stuck his head out, and called, "Breia! Breia, this way!"

Johnny said, "I don't really think that's how it wor—"

"Our room has a balcony!" Kiley eureka-shouted. "We'll take her right out there. C'mon, Joe, pick her up. Bring her along, come on." Then she led the charge to the corner suite.

Maya was a little jealous as they stampeded through it. Jack's ex was clearly giving him preferential treatment. The suite had a separate sitting room, kitchenette with a microwave and coffee maker, and yes, French doors that opened onto a balcony. Kiley ran ahead and opened them. Maya hurried right behind her, right beside Joe, spotting him in case he dropped Breia. He was so tall, and she would break so easily.

She was no longer mad at Breia. She was just scared for her and filled with a surge of protectiveness. The newbie felt like a little sister now.

Joe carried Breia out onto the patio, looked around, then lowered her body into a cushioned chair. "Someone bring a blanket."

"Joe, it's eighty out here."

"A *light* blanket."

Kiley rolled her eyes but went to the closet. "This thing's full of options." She pulled a blanket down. "Here, this is light and airy, but cozy soft."

She passed the thin, plaid blanket out to Joe on the balcony.

Maya stood back, just inside the French doors, watching him. He knelt down to put the blanket over her rather than bending that far. There was something unspeakably tender in the way he did it. She couldn't put her finger on which touch, which motion, which expression on his face gave that impression. Maybe it was all of them combined, or maybe it was just a feeling.

What if Joe *liked* Breia? Had her stupid ruse prevented him from acting on that? How could she not have seen it before now?

She felt eyes on her. Johnny's. She knew it before she looked back at him. He was coming toward her, and he said, "'Scuse me," as he went past her and out onto the patio. He leaned close said something soft near Joe's ear, and Joe shot Maya a look.

She closed her eyes, shook her head. Johnny was afraid Maya's feelings would be hurt by Joe's tenderness toward Breia. He was protective of her, despite being younger.

Too much younger.

Johnny straightened and turned to look out over the railing. "I don't think this is going to work. She's drawn back to her body. I don't think indoors or outdoors matters, really. She goes through walls."

"I thought you said she was corporeal," Maya said.

"On and off."

"Look!" Jack said, pointing past the patio in it's-a-bird-it's-a-plane fashion. "Holy, shit, *look*!"

They all did, and there was something—no, some*one* airborne hurtling toward them. It was Breia!

Maya blinked, rubbed her eyes and looked again. "Either they roofied my screwdriver on that boat, or Breia has wings."

"Yeah," Johnny said. "I was gonna mention that."

She didn't come to them, though, didn't even seem to see them standing there, instead she angled upward, to the third story. That part of the manse was a circular tower with glass all around. Everyone crowded onto the balcony, all craning their necks to see what she was doing up there. She fluttered around like a moth near a flame, and then she flew out a few yards, and shot back toward the house again. She hit the glass, flattened against it, and slid slowly downward. And she kept on sliding. Maya realized she hadn't hit the glass at all. She'd hit something outside the glass, some invisible barrier she couldn't pass through. And apparently it enveloped the entire place, because she slid right past them. She saw them, saw her own body beyond them, in the bed. Her eyes widened, she thumped a fist on the unseen barrier, and then pushed off and flew away.

"I don't think she can get back to her body," Maya said. "There's an some kind of energy field around this place, something that's keeping her out."

"That's a leap," Joe said.

Kiley elbowed him in the ribcage. "You just *saw* her hit something like a bug hitting a windshield. There's an invisible barrier. What we call it doesn't matter. You can do the math on that later. Right now, we need to get Breia back into her body."

"All right, all right, we can fix this," Joe said. "Common sense dictates, we just take her outside. Right? That'll work, won't it?" He was asking everyone, his gaze sliding from one person to the next.

Johnny looked at Maya with concern—all because he thought her boyfriend Joe—which he wasn't—was showing his feelings for another woman right in front of her—which he was. God, she had to tell him the truth about her and Joe, and soon.

"It seems like it should work, yes," Maya said. "But the bigger question here is why? Why is there an energy barrier around this place? Who put it there and for what purpose?"

Kiley rubbed her arms as if a chill had passed through her body, and looked down at the front pocket of her jeans, where the golden compact was tucked. It was open with its bottom in the pocket, and its mirrored top face-out. "Lady El says we can't trust anyone here until we know who did this and why. It would take powerful magic, she says."

Everyone nodded in agreement. Maya said, "So we don't want to let anyone find out about Breia's ...thing. We should handle this discreetly."

"Yes, yes, that's dead-on balls-accurate," Kiley said nodding. "All right. I have a plan."

She was an amazing leader, though a reluctant one. She fell into the role automatically, but didn't like when the gang acknowledged it. Too much pressure, Maya figured.

"Let's hear it," Jack said.

"The rest of us will clean up and go down to dinner as planned." Kiley said. "Joe, you stay here with Breia. We'll say she's still not feeling up to snuff and that we didn't want to leave her alone. A little while after we go down, get her body the hell out of this house. Through a back door or something, and try not to be seen. Find someplace safe to put her, and stay with her until she's back in her body. We don't know what kind of animals might be out there."

"Got it. I'll do a quick excursion to locate the best exit," he said.

"Good plan." Jack nodded his approval.

Johnny seemed to agree and Maya said, "Um, listen guys, I think we might be into something way bigger than we were led to believe here. First, as Lady El pointed out, somebody has cast some heavy-duty magic around this mansion. We need to find out who and why. And second, if Breia's trying to get in here, all winged-out for action, that suggests somebody around here is dead."

"Somebody on the third floor," Kiley said.

Once again, they all leaned out from the balcony and looked up.

"I think maybe Julie's dearly departed husband, isn't quite so departed after all," Maya said.

"So *Julie* didn't lie about that," Kiley said as if the name tasted sour on her lips. "Only the fact that he's apparently being kept here against his will."

KILEY TOOK the first post-flight shower to scrub off all the people-germs. She tended to feel the need to shower after any encounter with large groups of strangers, and she didn't even think it was all that OCD, given the world in which she currently lived.

Jack didn't sneak in to join her, though, even though the shower was huge, with terra cotta tiles and multiple heads. He was giving her time, which was exactly what she'd asked him to do. So being miserable about it was probably stupid. But she was miserable about it anyway.

Why couldn't he have just told her he'd been married? Why did he have to let this awfulness happen between them? Why had she insisted on coming here to begin with?

You know perfectly well why, Lady El said. *You have to be sure before you can get past this thing. You have to see them together, just like you told Jack. It's the only way your jealous, suspicious heart can let it go and start to trust him again."*

"You're mostly right."

I'm entirely right. And I know you've been burned before. I mean,

I wasn't there for it, but I know it. I saw you, when you first moved into my house, you know. All mopey and miserable, not to mention humiliated. You felt like a sap for believing in that con-man who took the goodies and left you high and dry. And you were out to prove Jack was just like him.

She blinked three times and said, "I was, wasn't I?"

But you couldn't. Because Jack isn't like him at all.

The golden compact was open and resting on the sink for ease of conversation. It was probably weird the way Kiley wrapped herself in a towel before stepping out of the delicious shower stall. Was she really shy about a ghost seeing her naked? She wrapped up in one of the sheet-sized towels, and came out. "You're pretty good. Maybe you should've been a therapist."

Oh honey, lounge singers are therapists. So are spiritual advisors for that matter. You ought know that by now, working with the dead and the bereaved.

Kiley looked for a label on the plush towel so she could shop for the brand, but there was none to be found. Sighing, she tugged it tight and returned to the bedroom.

Jack smiled when she came out, but his eyes wouldn't hold hers, and she thought he was feeling the awkwardness between them as much as she was. The distance, the sudden weirdness. Should he flirt, should he not, should he even hold her gaze very long?

Yeah, she got it. She *hated* it, but she got it.

Jack took his turn in the bathroom, and when the door closed on him, Kiley combed her hair into a sleek ponytail and skipped the makeup altogether. Moisturizer with sunblock was, she thought, the more sensible choice for a poolside dinner in a tropical paradise.

She pawed through her suitcase for something to wear and got dressed in a pair of light cotton shorts and a powder blue tank top with paint-stroke flower petals of orange and green across the front. She put her big sunglasses on her head, and for good measure, she put her bathing suit into a little woven bag. Then she grabbed the compact and tucked it into the shorts front pocket, once again leaving the mirrored part sticking out, facing forward.

Lady El's big red curls were held up high by a paisley print scarf. Her lashes had pink tips. No cigarette at the moment. She said, "Thanks for not closing me up. Despite Julie and whatever shenanigans are happening here, it's too gorgeous not to see. And I can't remember the last time I actually got out of the house."

"Are you actually stuck in the compact when it's closed?" Kiley asked, thinking that would be awful.

No, hon, I just pop back home until you open it again.

"That's a relief. Listen, do you have any input on all this stuff? Breia being some kind death fairy? Getting sucked out of her body when someone needs help crossing over?"

Yes. I have very important input. You should keep her far away from me!

Kiley tilted her head and said, "She's never popped out of her body or sprouted wings around you, though. That alone should tell us something."

Like what?

"God, El, I was hoping you could tell me! You're the one who's dead."

That was uncalled for.

"Sorry. But maybe it does mean something. I mean, it has to mean something, right? Maybe it's because you're not stuck."

A ghost needs a body to inhabit, Lady El said. Her cigarette had re-appeared in its foot-long white holder. She blew a puff of smoke and it smelled like lavender and Kiley wondered briefly whether she could switch up the scent on demand. Maybe go for some cinnamon spice or sandalwood every once in a while.

Apparently El heard the thought, because she rolled her eyes, puffed again, and it smelled like strawberry. *We all saw what happened to Breia's parents when they hung around too long in the physical world without a physical form, right?* she asked.

"Right."

But that didn't happen to me. I've been around for decades. Died in sixty-nine. I think it's because I attached my soul to my house—to something physical. A soul needs a physical body to remain in the physical world.

"Okay," Kiley said, turning that over in her mind and trying to keep up with Lady El's logic.

Maybe the death fairy is only drawn to souls without a body, free-floating phantasms.

"Isn't that from *Ghostbusters*?"

From what, now?

"Never mind." Kiley made a mental note to play the film for Lady El when they got back home. She would love it. "I like your theory. So let's see if you can go two for two. Why do you think there's a magical barrier around this place?"

Lady El tapped her chin with her cigarette holder, then opened her fingers and it vanished. Convenient. *There are only two reasons I can think of. Someone either wants to keep non-physical beings out, or they want to keep them in. Has to be one or the other.*

"Well, maybe we're about to find out. We'll keep Julie distracted while Joe takes Breia outside so she can get back into her body. And maybe I can shake Julie into slipping up and revealing something at dinner." She set the compact on the dresser, open, and hung the rest of her clothes in the closet.

Then she decided to do the same for Jack just to be nice. She unzipped his duffel, and pulled out a stack of folded clothes from which a small box fell. A small square box. The kind that usually held jewelry. More specifically, the kind that usually held a ring.

"Holy shit," she whispered.

Hallelujah! El shouted.

The sudden cessation of running water sounds startled Kiley so much she dropped the clothes on the floor, then fell to her knees and gathered them up, quickly shoving them back into his unzipped duffel. She reached for the ring—if it was a ring, it might not be a ring, maybe a little pair of earrings or something —she shouldn't just assume it was a ring. There it was. Under the bed. She must have kicked it. She flattened to her stomach, reached under the bed, closed her hand around the ring, shoved it into the duffel. The bathroom door was opening. She pivoted just as Jack came out with a towel knotted around his hips.

He looked at her, standing awkwardly beside the bed in front of his unzipped and ransacked duffel. The clothes inside were a mess now. He was sure to notice that. Maybe she could blame it on the airline.

Damn, it was a carry-on.

"Um, how do I look?" She spread her arms, gave a spin, and knocked the duffel off the bed as deliberately as a cat clearing a coffee table. It landed upside down on the floor exactly as she had intended. "Oh, crap, I'm sorry!"

That was quick thinking, El clapped her hands like an enthusiastic audience member at a Lady El performance. *Brava. Brava!*

Jack grabbed her around the waist, pulled her close and turned around, so she was facing away from the bed when he let her go. "You look gorgeous. You always look gorgeous. But you probably need shoes." He pointed toward the closet, then bent to retrieve his bag while her back was to him.

Ohh, he's pretty smooth, too, isn't he?

"Shoes. Right." She went to the closet and chose a pair of strappy sandals, giving Jack time to scramble for his clothes and her ring. If it was a ring, and if it was for her. It could be for anyone. Hell, it might be some old thing he was returning to

Julie for all she knew. She waited until she heard the zipper before turning to face him again.

If you don't want him to know you know, sister, you'd better turn down the headlights. You're beaming at him the way I beam at chocolate cake.

Kiley blinked and tried to wipe the goofy smile off her face. Jack got dressed, casual shorts and a floral print button-down he'd probably picked up just for the trip.

MAYA MET Johnny in the hall outside her room. He wore cargo shorts and a short-sleeved, flower-printed "tourist" shirt. She'd changed into an airy sundress and she'd brought a bathing suit in her shoulder bag. Before they'd done more than look each other up and down, the corner suite's door opened, and Jack and Kiley came out. Jack was wearing a very similar shirt.

"Did you guys consult on wardrobe, or what?" Maya asked.

Joe opened the door to Breia's room, but had obviously visited his own. His close-cropped hair was still wet from a recent shower, and his floral print button down was sticking to his damp skin.

"You *did* consult on clothes, didn't you?" Maya asked.

Johnny shrugged and Joe just looked confused.

"How's our girl doing?" Kiley asked. "Any change?"

"No," Joe said. "But she's been flitting around that third level again and I'm quite concerned that someone else will see her. We should work from the assumption that she's not only visible to us, but to anyone who happens to look up."

Kiley looked down at the compact, whose mirror was sticking up out of the front pocket of her cute shorts. "What do you mean, El?" She asked the mirror. Then she looked up. "Lady El says Breia shouldn't be out of her body too long."

"I predict it won't be much longer, if it works the way we theorize it does," Joe said with a look at Johnny.

"Why don't *you* go down to dinner, Joe?" he asked. "Let me take Breia outside." Johnny's question was so off topic that it got everyone's attention.

"It's fine, Johnny." Maya touched his arm when she said it, and he had to have felt the pulse that went through them both at that slight contact. Her palm pressed to his bicep. He looked at her, his eyes searching hers, so she said it again. "It's really okay."

"Okay."

"Take good care of her, Joe. See you later," Maya said, then she looked past him, through the open door. "You, too, Breia. I hope."

"I hope so, too," Joe said, then he closed the door.

The four of them headed to the impressive staircase and then down it and across the expansive foyer. Their steps echoed on the tiled floor, and a row of glass panes faced outward toward the veranda and the pools beyond.

Maya leaned forward, squinting. "Ah, some of these panes open. I get it," she said, then she pushed on one of the panes, and lo and behold, it swung open. She was relieved. It would've been embarrassing if the thing hadn't budged. They all stepped out onto the veranda, but there was no one near the pools there.

"Ahh, you must be the new guests," said a middle-aged woman in immaculate white shorts and shirt. Another employee, obviously, although this one wore an equally spotless white apron over her clothes. "I'm Beasley, the cook. You are looking for the dinner party, yes?" The blond hair, the deep tan, the white teeth must all be part of the uniform too. She was middle aged, not young like yacht-pilot Kevin, and she had an accent that sounded slightly Nordic.

"We were told to come to the pool," Kiley said.

Maya was still mulling on the words "dinner party."

"Of course, but not this one. Follow me." With that accent, her name should've been Helga or Elsa, Maya thought. Beasley guided them along the veranda and down its side stairs to ground level, where a flawless flagstone walk led around the place, across groomed lawns with islands of flowering plants. Not a single weed poked out of a single white gravel bed.

The walkway curved again around the rear of the house, where a two-level deck became a stone patio that bordered a gigantic kidney-shaped pool. At one end, a waterfall plummeted from a twenty-foot monolith. There was a cave behind the cascade that you could swim through. Around the pool, umbrella tables with upright chairs, and long, lazy beach chairs awaited occupants, and there was a long table that looked out of place near the end of the patio. Uniformed staff were loading it with food.

"There you are!" Julie hurried over, white high-heels clacking, white clothes flowing in the breeze. She surely loved white. Behind her, a woman and a man who were clearly not servants, rose from the chairs where they'd been sitting. The elderly woman swam in her sari and wore her white hair long and loose. The man was short and round and wore a white linen suit with a Panama hat and wire-rimmed glasses.

"Everyone, these are the people I was telling you about," Julie said. "Jack, Kiley, Johnny, and Maya." Then she frowned. "Where are the others? I hope your friend is better."

"She is," Kiley said. "But she wasn't up to dinner. Joe didn't want to leave her alone."

"He's very devoted. I could see it the day I first met you all."

Kiley and Maya exchanged a surprised look, and Johnny kind of winced and lowered his head.

Julie went on. "Forgive me. I'm easily distracted these days. These are Arthur's closest friends, Matilda Carlise and Horace Stoltz. They're here to help in any way they can."

Maya wondered just what it was the two strangers thought they might be able to do to help. Then she caught sight of the view in the distance, and she forgot about everything else. "Will you just look at that?" she asked no one in particular.

Kiley looked, then adjusted the compact in her pocket, and Maya knew she was making sure Lady El could see the spectacular vista. The trees had been cut and trimmed in such a way that the view of the ocean off the eastern side of the island, the side that faced away from the coast, was unobstructed. The elevation of the mansion was far higher than it had at first seemed. That became clear when you saw the rocky drop downward to the Atlantic. A path led down amongst the rocks to the beach below. There were woods flanking it on either side. And beyond the beach, nothing but water and twilight sky as far as the eye could see.

"If you get up early, you can watch the sunrise from here," Julie said. "It was one of Arthur's favorite things about this place."

"Your late husband," Kiley said.

Julie nodded. "He was a painter, you know. He painted more sunrises than I can count. The last few months of his life, though, he barely left his studio." She turned to gaze upward at the house as she said it, and they all did, too.

"His studio. Is that what's on the third floor?" Maya asked.

"Yes, how did you know?" Julie asked.

Maya said, "If I were an artist, that's where I'd want to be. It's like the top part of a lighthouse, isn't it? But bigger. All those windows all the way around."

Kiley said, "I'd love to see it. We all would."

"It's the first thing I want to show you," Julie said. "It's the place he loved best inside the house. But after dinner."

CHAPTER 6

Kiley carried her plate along the buffet, helping herself to everything that looked good—and everything looked good. Or at least it did until Maya leaned in close and whispered, "Do you think we can trust the food?"

"Do you think she lured us out here to poison us?"

"Or drug us or induce hallucinations."

"But why?" Kiley asked. "What would be the point?"

Maya shrugged, looking at the people sharing breakfast with them, one by one. "Who knows why? Same reason somebody put an energetic barrier around this place, I imagine. A strong one."

"Oh, come on, as strong as yours?"

"Stronger, maybe. I don't know."

"Yours kept out a pair of raging, powerful entities determined to get past it," Kiley reminded her.

Excuse me? The ghost in the gold compact seemed to have taken offense.

"With a little help from Lady El, I mean," Kiley added. "I doubt this barrier cold be any stronger than yours."

"Well, it's definitely darker than mine," Maya replied.

"Shit." Kiley scanned the plates of those already at their tables, digging in.

Horace Stoltz had taken off his Panama hat to reveal the finest case of male pattern baldness Kiley had ever seen. The hair around the outside was two inches too long and dyed horseshoe black. He tended to show his bottom teeth when he smiled or spoke, and they were small, like the teeth of a child.

Tilda Carlisle was an actress who'd been murdered in a series of teenage slasher films back in the seventies. Now she was best known for a series of commercials spoofing those same films for a bank or a credit card or something.

Kiley thought even at sixty-something, she was still stunning. It wasn't just physical beauty, though. It was her presence. Or something.

I get it, Lady El said from her open compact mirror. *It's her energy. It's very much like my own, when I perform.*

Kiley rolled her eyes at the vanity of the statement, and it was fine, because she wasn't looking in the mirror. She hadn't quite figured out if the two were a couple or what their deal was, other than being two of Arthur's best friends.

She reached into her straw bag for her sunglasses, and readjusted Lady El's angle without being obvious about it. She'd had to move the gold compact out of her pocket to sit, but found a pocket in the purse to be just as handy.

"You're holding up the line," Maya said, nudging her. Jack had been right ahead of her, but he was already at a little table with his plate.

"Eat what they eat," Kiley said. "And especially what Julie eats."

"Julie's eating meat," Maya said. "Imma take my chances with the veggies."

Kiley chose a few things with great care, but only things

she'd seen other people eat, and then she headed for the table where Jack waited, leaned in and told him to do the same.

Horace was at their small round table. Julie was at the table right beside theirs with Tilda. Johnny and Maya sat down in the two empty chairs there.

Small talk ensued. Tilda was full of questions about Spook Central, what they did, how it all worked. Kiley ate, and the food was so good, she wanted to try all the things she'd left behind.

Eventually, she leaned back in her chair, and said, "I am definitely not going swimming for at least, what?"

"An hour." Jack answered instantly and grinned at her. The lines were Billy Crystal and Carol Caine's from *The Princess Bride*, one of her favorite flicks.

Horace smiled at them as if he were looking at a cute puppy. "You two are precious together. God I want that."

Kiley cleared her throat and yanked her eyes away from her man. She wasn't quite finished being mad at him yet, but he was melting her with his smile. He'd reminded her, just then, how close they'd grown since they'd been living together.

But this wasn't the time or place to focus on relationship issues.

"So, Julie," Kiley said, "Is it okay to talk business at this meal?"

"It's not business, though, is it?" she asked in return. "It couldn't be more personal. And yes, they know why you're here. They're his best friends. Met in a support group. I thought their presence here might help you contact him."

"To ask him about the missing jewelry" Kiley said.

"Yes." She lowered her head. "And to help him cross over, of course."

"Oh look! Are these the stragglers we've been hearing about?" Horace said, flashing his baby teeth in his round, little boy face.

Joe and Breia came walking out of the woods toward the tables, and Kiley noticed immediately that something was off. Joe looked normal, but Breia, back in her body and conscious, thank goodness, was smiling too widely and blinking too much.

"Hello again, Joe," Julie said. "I hope you're feeling better, Breia."

"Much better, thank you. A walk in the fresh air did me a world of good."

"As it always does for me," she said. "Just make sure you stick to the road. There are all manner of hazards in the woods. Poisonous plants, wild boar, murder hornets." She smiled and closed her eyes. "That was what Arthur called them, anyway."

"He was such a drama queen," said Tilda, who was technically an *actual* a drama queen.

Horace chuckled as if a happy memory had crossed his mind.

"Horace, Tilda, these are Joe and Breia. Obviously. Help yourself to food, you two."

"Oh, I'll show you what you have to try." Kiley got up from her chair and grabbed one of their elbows with each hand, walking between them to the buffet table. And then, through a clenched-teeth smile, she asked, "What's wrong?"

"We found a fresh grave in the woods," Breia whispered.

"And there's still no cell service, even this close to the house," Joe put in. "We'll have to hook up to their wireless, ASAP. Ask for the password, okay?"

"Sure, yeah, but who cares about having zero bars? You found a freaking grave?"

"We found freshly turned earth," Joe said, "mounded up in a roughly rectangular shape."

"A human-sized rectangular shape," Breia added.

"But we don't *know* it's a grave," Joe went ont. "And if it is, we don't know it's a human being who's buried there. It might be a pet."

"Right, a pet with the exact dimensions of a human." Breia looked up quickly. "Sorry, Joe, but there's a body in that hole."

"Your death fairy sense tingling, is it?" Kiley asked.

"No." She tilted her head to one side. "Maybe."

"Maybe?"

"Yeah, maybe."

"They're looking at us," Joe said, and he started loading up a plate. "What the hell is Jack's ex up to, here, anyway?"

"Eat what they eat, just in case," Kiley said. "We'll check out the grave later."

"Get the wireless password," Joe said.

"Yes, Joe, I'll get the wireless password. You'll be reconnected to the outside world in no time." Kiley headed back to the table, pasting a great big smile on her face. She sat in her seat and said, "So Julie, I have two questions. First, what's the wifi password, and second, why is there an energy barrier around your house?"

Jack choked on his drink and Maya dropped her fork. It clattered against her plate. They both sent her what-the-fuck-are-you-doing looks.

"Energy barrier?" *Julie* blinked her baby blues. "I don't even know what that is." As she said it, she sought help from Jack with her eyes, which made Kiley want to poke them with something sharp.

Joe said, "The wifi password, then. That's an easy one, right?"

"What do you mean, Kiley?" Julie asked. "Please explain."

Kiley opened her palm toward Maya, like an emcee throwing to the next presenter. Maya swallowed her food, dabbed her lips with a napkin, and took a sip of water before she spoke. "People with ...magical skills can create energetic spheres around areas they wish to protect. They can be designed to can keep energy and energetic beings from passing through.

"Energetic beings." Julie repeated the words as if they were from another language.

"Non-physical entities," Maya said.

"Ghosts," Kiley clarified.

"Or other non-physical beings." Maya slanted a look at Breia. "The thing is, some of us can sense such barriers, and you have one. A powerful one."

"That's why Arthur's stuck here," Breia said. "His spirit can't get out. The barrier is holding him in. It's ...well, frankly, it's cruel. And it's not going to go very well for very long. You can trust me on that."

"Then ...Arthur *is* here" Julie said. She sent a terrified look at her home. "And you're saying he's trapped here?"

Maya said, "Well, we *think* he might be—"

"We know for sure he is," Breia interrupted. "I saw him myself."

"That's awful!" Horace threw down his napkin.

"It's heartbreaking." Tears pooled in Tilda's eyes. "Our poor Arthur."

"How could such a thing get there?" Julie asked. "And how do we get rid of it so my husband can be at peace?" She sent her pleading gaze to Jack again. "You have to talk to him, Jack. If anyone knows more about this thing, it would be Arthur. I need you to communicate with him."

"We've only just got here," Jack said. "We'll need a little time to figure things out. And yes, I'll do my best to contact Arthur." He made his voice all strong and confident, the way he did when trying to soothe Kiley through a scary situation. She hated that he used that tone for *Julie.*

Joe held up his phone. "We could do some online research

that might help. What did you say that wifi password was again?"

Julie shifted her eyes sideways at him. "There's no internet out here. Arthur wouldn't allow it. This was his refuge."

Joe deflated visibly.

Horace Stoltz lifted his glass and altered his voice, Kiley presumed in an imitation of Arthur Kendall. "What good is a refuge from the world if you invite the world in with you?"

"Hear, hear," Tilda said, and tapped his glass with hers. They both sipped, and then she went on. "At least, if Arthur is trapped, he's trapped in the place he loved best. I don't think it's all that tragic."

"That's because you've never dealt with a ghost stuck in the physical world before," Breia said. She looked at her fellow scoops and every one of them nodded.

Julie rubbed her arms as if she were suddenly cold.

CHAPTER 7

"**A** nd this," Julie said, opening a large door some time later, "was Arthur's space."

Maya opened her senses wide. They'd entered the corner suite on the second floor's west wing. Their own rooms were all in the east wing, and the two were separated by the split staircase.

Julie had led them through the entire house, and had saved the most interesting parts for last. Tilda and Horace, her other guests, had begged off, saying they knew the entire island by heart. Breia had stayed behind with Joe to make use of the pool, so she wouldn't inadvertently blip out of her body in the presence of dead Arthur's living wife.

Maya had tried to feel the energy of each part of the house as they'd moved through it, with little success. That is, until she'd stepped into the corner suite. In there, a static charge zigzagged along the nape of her neck, causing the fine hairs to stand on end.

"Tell us about Arthur," she said, but she was tuning in Arthur's energy more than his widow's words.

She met Johnny's eyes, and he gave a slight nod to tell her he was feeling it, too, and then they both looked at Jack. He was skimming the place with probing eyes, every corner, the closet, the bed, all without moving from the spot where he stood.

"He was a lot older than me," Julie said. "A lot of people accused me of being after his money, but that was never what it was about. I'll probably never live it down, though, especially since he left me everything in the will."

"That's difficult for you, I'm sure," Maya said. "But tell us about *Arthur*." She kept her voice and her eyes soft, not wanting to piss the woman off so soon. Still, she needed to guide the woman onto the right topic. Talking about Arthur would align them with his spirit, and make communication easier.

There was a restless beauty to Arthur's energy. She sensed his powerful creativity, his curious mind, and the unpleasant static buzz of his impatience and frustration.

"Yeah," Julie said, smiling back, lowering her eyes. "You're right. This isn't about me. Arthur ..." She looked around his rooms and sighed. Her grief seemed genuine. She clearly missed him. "He was an artist, you know. Everybody remembers him as this media mogul, but all he ever wanted to do was paint. He was the happiest retiree you could meet."

She went on, talking about Arthur's healthy lifestyle, age notwithstanding; his morning swims, his daily jogs around the island. While she spoke, Maya moved around the living room part of the suite, trailing a hand over the dark furniture, noticing the antique desk, the big screen TV on the wall, the wet bar, the comfortable furnishings. The most curious thing was a perfectly vertical spiral staircase. It was black wrought iron, with vines and leaves in its twisting rail.

She tried to complete her inspection of the room, but that staircase kept pulling her gaze back. She noted an adjoining door that led to a bathroom, another to a bedroom that felt as if it hadn't been used in a long time. "He didn't sleep in here," she said softly.

"Wow, you can tell that?" Julie's brows rose high. "It's true, he didn't. He told us that once he became bedridden, he wanted to be in his studio. And honestly, I think he's still there. You confirmed it for me at dinner. I was so sure you'd think I was crazy." Julie's eyes flicked to Jack when she said it, and Maya shot a look Kiley's way. Yep, she'd noticed. "I didn't believe in these kinds of things myself until now. And I didn't know who to turn to. But I did know that my Jack—"

Her Jack? Kiley said it with her eyes, and Maya heard it loud and clear.

"—was always an honest man." Julie gazed at him like he was the second coming. "If you say you can talk to the dead, then you can. Contacting you was the easiest way to rule out charlatans and frauds. If anyone can reach Arthur, you can, Jack. I believe in you."

Jack had moved closer to the spiral staircase, and Maya could've sworn he was oblivious to all Julie's praise. Without asking permission, he started up, disappearing through the top, and then after a moment, he said, "You guys should come up here."

Kiley was already halfway. Johnny stood at the bottom, but motioned at Maya to go ahead of him, so she did, and he followed.

Maya realized Johnny could see right up her sundress if he tipped his head back. Instead, he put his hands on the backs of her thighs, holding the fabric in place while she climbed.

She emerged into the circular room at the top of the mansion. The top step was at floor level, with its vine-twisted railing extending upward. The room was round and completely surrounded in glass. On closer inspection, a pair of the glass panes turned out to be sliding doors that led onto the wrap-around deck.

"Wow," Maya said, walking to the glass, and then slowly around the whole room to take in the view. It was already dark, but the moon illuminated the entire island and the ocean that surrounded it.

The space was littered with easels and canvases and drafting tables. A large wooden cube-like desk, solid to the floor on all four sides, was covered in paints and brushes and rags. One stand held a mini-fridge. Canvas upon canvas leaned everywhere. Some were finished, some were blank, and some were at various stages in-between. They were all different, and yet the same. The ocean and the sky and the island beyond the windows, sometimes bright and sunny, sometimes overcast and moody, sometimes dark and stormy. There were sunrises and sunsets, moonrises and moonsets, too, in every phase. There were choppy waves and glass-smooth seas. There were still trees, and trees bent and whipped by winds.

It broke Maya's heart a little to realize this had been Arthur Kendall's entire life for a time. Then again, if you had to die, this was a beautiful place for it.

On one side of the circle, there was an unmade hospital bed, its blankets and sheets as rumpled as if its owner had just got up out of it. It was a small bed, and even then they'd probably had to bring it up here in pieces and put it together in the room. There was a wheelchair beside it, and an IV pole with an empty bag. It didn't feel as if anyone had been in the room since Arthur had passed away.

"How long since he died?" Maya asked. She opened the mini-fridge, saw small glass medicine vials inside. It was obvious that no one had done much to this room since Arthur's death.

"Two weeks," Julie replied.

"He's here, I feel him," Johnny said.

"He's standing on the deck ignoring us," Jack said, pointing. "Right out there."

Maya looked, they all did, but only Jack could see the guy. Julie made a sound that could only be described as a whimper, and gazed through the glass doors with tears welling anew. "Can you talk to him, Jack?" It was a plea. She moved to the glass and pressed her hands to it.

"I can try, Jack said.

"Lady El will try, too," Kiley whispered, but for Maya's ears alone. She'd been carrying that golden compact around everywhere she went, open with the mirror part facing out. Maya thought Kiley was developing quite a friendship with Spook Central's house ghost.

"I wish I could see him," Julie said from near the glass.

"I'll narrate as best I can," Jack said. He slid the glass door open, and stepped out onto the deck. An ocean breeze came in, sweeping the old, stale air from the room. Maya thought the atmosphere grew lighter by a metaphysical ton.

"Hey, Arthur. I'm Jack. I'm here to help."

Everyone looked on. It looked for all the world as if Jack were speaking to thin air, but Maya knew better.

"I'm aware there's some kind of barrier keeping you here. I promise, we're going to figure out how to take it down, so your spirit can fly free."

Jack waited in silence, gazing at nothing.

"Is he ...saying anything?" Julie asked. She sagged a little, and grabbed hold of the bed rail to catch herself.

"He's not listening to me. He seems angry and frustrated. Wait, he might be coming around. He's turning toward us." Jack was smiling, then his face changed. He reached behind him and pushed Julie back inside, just before something hit like wrecking ball. He landed on his back and slid over the wooden deck, toward the railings.

"Jesus!" Kiley shoved past Julie to get out there, planted herself between Jack and the force that had hit him and screamed, "Knock it the fuck off, asshole!"

Jack stopped sliding, having wrapped one hand around the railing behind him. "He's gone. It's okay. I'm okay."

"Fucking ghosts anyway. Honest to Christ I don't know why we bother helping them." Kiley's voice was shaking. Maya could hear it. She turned to clasp Jack's hand and help him up.

"Gone where?" Julie asked.

"Nowhere, really, when it comes down to it," Jack said. "He's still here. Just not on a wavelength where I can reach him."

"That is amazing, that you can do that," Kiley said, a little awe in her voice for the skills of her man. A little ripple of warmth formed in Maya's chest. They'd be okay, those two.

"Do you think maybe," Julie asked, "he doesn't *want* to leave?" She sounded as if she hoped he would answer yes.

Jack shrugged. "I don't know. All I got from him was anger."

Julie closed her eyes, then turned, and left the room, hurrying down the spiral stairs, one hand to her lips, obviously too upset to remain in her dead husband's studio.

"Do you really believe *Julie* was completely unaware of this energy barrier thingie?" Kiley asked anyone close enough to hear her.

"It didn't just appear by accident," Maya said. "*Somebody* cast it."

"But maybe not her," Jack said. Kiley glared at him, but he just shrugged. "She said he left her everything. He's gone. She's a rich widow. What reason would she have to keep him trapped here?"

"What reason would anybody else have?" Kiley countered.

Jack only shrugged, but Johnny said, "When we figure out why, that'll tell us who. But research is gonna be tough without internet or even a freaking phone."

Kiley paced, head down, then nodded. "Okay, here's what we'll do. We'll take the boat back to the mainland in the morning, make up some errand we need to run or something. We'll do some further research on reasons to hold a soul captive and maybe how to remove powerful energy barriers, and then we come back."

"Maybe Joe can even find a satellite phone while we're there," Maya said. "He's going a little crazy without an internet connection—as tech geeks do. But research is the main thing."

Johnny glanced down the stairway, then in a low voice said, "We have to tell the police about the body in the woods."

"We don't know that there *is* a body in the woods," Kiley reminded him. "Just a grave-shaped mound of dirt."

"Well, how *can* we be sure?" Maya countered. "Unless we dig it up, and we're certainly not doing that." She said it as if it was the obvious conclusion.

Then Johnny said, "It uh, wouldn't be the first time we've dug up a body."

"In the woods," Kiley added.

"In the dead of night," Jack put in.

"Fuck my life," said Maya, pressing a palm to her forehead and closing her eyes.

Johnny patted her on the shoulder, then gave it a squeeze that made her feel warm all over. She leaned into his touch. She didn't really mean to, she didn't try very hard not to, either.

"There's a gardener's shed around the west side of the yard," he said. "Probably shovels in there."

"All right, all right," Maya said, capitulating, but dreading the task ahead. "If we absolutely have to do this—"

"We do," Kiley said.

"—we'll sneak outside one or two at a time and meet at the gardener's shed at midnight."

Kiley widened her eyes. "Why the hell midnight?"

To which Maya replied, "Why the hell not?"

KILEY DID NOT OBJECT to the pure male chauvinism displayed by the guys taking turns with the two shovels. Johnny actually did most of the digging, referring to the other two as the "old dudes."

Silence hung heavy in the night. The birds were even quiet. The gang was quiet too, as they stood around an unmarked grave. A warm, salty breeze blew darkness through the woods, and in the distance the waves lapped the island's shore. The only other sound was the rhythmic digging. The soft sound of the shovel sinking into loose earth, then the even lighter *shoosh* of that dirt being dumped beside the grave. They were trying to keep it neat, so when they put everything back, it would look undisturbed. Kiley didn't think that was really possible, though.

Sink, pour, sink, pour. There should've been a chain gang making up lyrics to go with the work.

I don't like this, no not one bit, Lady El said.

"I thought you'd want to see. I can close you back up, if you want." Kiley reached for the compact, which was in the front pocket of her jeans, open, with the mirror facing out.

No, no, don't! El's objection was instant and passionate. *I mean, we've come this far. I might as well see what you uncover.*

"Yeah, that's what I thought you'd say."

"You know," Maya said to Kiley, "We'd never know if you had completely lost your mind and were suffering hallucinations, or if you were just conversing with your ghost."

"Oh, trust me," Kiley said, "If I go batshit, you're gonna know it."

Breia gave a soft, nervous laugh, and moved a little closer to Joe.

Johnny was standing knee-deep in the hole when he drove his shovel in, then stopped and made a face and said, "Oh, hell, I hit something soft."

Jack said, "I got it, I got it, make room for me." He extended his arm, and Kiley admired it. He'd rolled up his shirt sleeve to the elbow. Was it weird to find forearms sexy?

You got it bad, yet you insist on staying mad. Lady El snapped her fingers twice and said, *That's a song lyric if ever I heard one. And I've heard plenty.*

Johnny clasped Jack's forearm and climbed out of the hole they'd dug. Jack jumped in. He stood in one end, and used his shovel to scrape dirt away from around the blade of Johnny's shovel, which was standing upright. Then handed his shovel up, and once Joe took it from him, he bent down and brushed the dirt away with his hands instead.

"Fabric. A...a blanket, maybe." He kept brushing. "Yeah, okay, I don't know what it's covering, but the shovel went into it."

"Pull it out," Johnny said.

Jack straightened and grabbed the shovel's handle, then lifted it. Then he turned around, threw an arm over his face and swore. A second later, the smell reached the rest of them too.

"Definitely something dead," Joe said as Jack scrambled out of the hole.

"Well, jeez, guys, you quitting now?" Kiley said. "We have to know what or who that is down there." Then, "Oh for fuck's sake," and she jumped into the hole while Lady El shouted, *Nooooo!*

"Buck up, El. You can't be afraid of dead people when you are one."

She pulled her shirt up over her face, knelt at the end of the grave she hoped was the head, and started brushing dirt away. "Breia, we should keep gloves in our go-kits from now on. Make a note, will you?"

"Note taken. Grave-digging gloves in the go-kits. Maybe masks, too, if exhuming bodies is going to be a regular occurrence."

"You feeling any urge to sprout wings, Bray?" Maya asked.

"Nope. Whoever is down there has already crossed over."

"What the hell is that?" Kiley asked, feeling something hard, and brushing away more dirt from around the hard, curving thing. "Is that a horn?" The ridged, curved shape emerged from the head of... "A goat. It's a goat." She got hold of the horn, and tugged, and the head came almost all the way out of the dirt. There were wilted, brown flowers braided around the horns like a crown resting on the animal's head, and there was a wide gaping opening in the neck. "Looks like its throat has been cut."

"That's a sacrifice," Maya said. "Get out of there, Kiley. That's bad juju."

Jack reached down and helped pull Kiley out of the grave. Johnny said, "Think we need to exhume the body?"

"Cause of death is obvious," Joe said, shining his flashlight on the unearthed head of the poor creature. Its eyes were closed, thank goodness. "I think we've got all we're going to get from this excursion."

Jack nodded. "I concur, let's fill it in."

So the boys started putting the dirt back. As they worked, Breia knelt, pressed her hands to the ground, and said, "I'm so sorry you died in such a horrible way, goat. I'm glad you're at peace now."

"Me, too," Maya said, standing at her side, one hand on her shoulder.

When the grave was filled in, they all walked around it, brushing the loose earth out of the grasses and weeds and back into the grave by the tree-broken moonlight and the beams of their flashlights. Kiley hoped it would look undisturbed by day, but there was no way to be sure it would.

"I think we should take a boat and head back to the mainland now," Maya said. "There's some dark magic going on here. I
don't know who's behind it, but let's not be in the middle of it. I
think we should get the hell off this island tonight. We can
return Julie's deposit as soon as we get home."

Kiley studied her face, then nodded and looked at the others.
"What do you guys think?"

Jack said, "I'm not sure any of us are experienced enough at
piloting a boat to ensure we'd get back to the coast in one piece.
Or back to the coast at all. Especially by night."

"I don't know about that," Joe said. "If the boat has a compass
and we point ourselves west, we're going to hit the land sooner
or later. America's too big to miss."

"I've driven a boat or two in my time," Johnny said. "Little
speedboats, but still."

"That's good enough for me." Maya looked at the others.
"You all know my vote. What do you say?"

"I vote we leave right now," Breia said. "I don't even want to
go back for our stuff."

"All in favor?" Kiley asked. Seeing her little gang spooked
was more than she could take.

They all raised their hands.

"Okay, let's do it, then."

Jack led them through the woods at an angle he said he
thought would bring them out onto the road, and it did. They
followed it all the way back to the pier. The long, silent, empty
pier. Not one single boat remained.

CHAPTER 8

"I can't believe we're going to play it cool," Kiley said, lying wide awake in bed beside Jack later that night. "I think we should have pounded on Julie's bedroom door, dragged her out of bed, and demanded she explain what the hell happened to all the boats. Not to mention the poor freaking goat."

"Yeah, but nobody agreed with you. The vote was five-one."

"Five-two," she countered. "Lady El's on my side."

"She can't vote if you're the only one who can hear her."

"What, you don't trust me? You're the one with the secret, possibly demon-worshipping ex-wife."

He rolled over, choosing not to engage. They'd showered off the grave dirt and there were still a few hours left of the night. "We'll get to the bottom of this in the morning," he said. Kiley presumed he'd first taken a deep breath and counted to ten. "In the meantime, we should get some sleep."

"Sleep? How are we going to sleep—we are captives on a private island with no way off, in a magically-barricaded mansion with no cell service, no landline, an angry ghost, and a houseful of goat murderers."

"Alleged goat murderers." He pulled up the covers, and she

slid closer, because no matter how bad things were, being all up against him skin to skin in bed was good. Beyond good. She wrapped her arms around him.

He hugged pulled her arms around his waist and snuggled closer. "Does this mean I'm forgiven?"

"No."

"I'll take it anyway."

"Yeah, you will," she said, and bit his shoulder blade.

He rolled over quick and pulled her close. "I promise you, this isn't as bad as it seems."

"No," she said. "I'm sure it's probably way worse."

His reply didn't come for several long seconds, and when it did, it was unintelligible and pillow-muffled. He was already asleep, and all the hugging in the world wasn't going to soothe her enough to let her get there with him.

She slid out of bed, pulled on her spa robe, and tied its sash. The thing was heavy, as if weighted, and she found that comforting, even on a warm night like this one. She stepped into her fluffy penguin slippers and started to leave the room, then went to her nightstand and picked up the compact. She didn't open it until she was in the hall with the door closed.

Lady El was in red satin pajamas with black piping and iridescent buttons, maybe mother-of-pearl.

Opal, dear. I do not sleep with seafood on my chest. She tugged the knot in the top of her satin hair wrap and said, *What are we doing up at this ungodly hour?*

"Investigating. That's what investigators do."

You're not a PI, you're a ghost-hunter.

"Same thing, though, isn't it?" She tucked the bottom half of the compact into her robe's sash, so El would be able to see, and started down the hallway.

Where are we going?

"Downstairs," she whispered. "There's certainly no point

poking around up here. Julie wouldn't have put us in the same wing with her secrets."

Fuck Julie and her secrets, El said. Because that was what girlfriends did. They hated the same bitches you did, solely because you did. *I want you to come home.*

"I want us to come home, too."

In the meantime, I want you to promise me that if you die, you will close this compact before you breathe your last, so I don't wind up stuck here with the goat-murderers.

"You have my word."

Tell the others, just in case you die first.

"You're so upbeat and encouraging." Kiley stopped walking and sniffed the air. "I smell incense." They were in front of Maya's door. "Of course I smell incense." Dancing yellow light came beneath the crack. Maya was moving around in there, so she tapped the door softly.

"Who's there?" Maya called.

"It's me."

The door opened. Maya stood in it, wearing a deep red robe that might've been satin, with black lace trim on the sleeves and collar. Her hair was down. Man, if Johnny saw her like this, he'd melt into a puddle on the floor.

"Come on in." Maya stepped aside.

Kiley walked in. The bed was still made. There were five lit candles in a circle on the floor, a blue glass bottle with its cork out, a little jar with something white inside—sugar? Salt? An incense cone sat atop an impossibly dainty ceramic holder, releasing a spiral of fragrant smoke. It smelled like magic and mystery to Kiley.

"I didn't mean to interrupt."

"I was trying to connect with my guides. See if they knew anything. But this place ..." She shook her head. "It's stupid."

"It's not stupid. Tell me."

Yes, spill it!

"You know how there's no cell service here?"

Kiley nodded.

"It feels like that's not the only connection that's down in this place."

Kiley searched inwardly for the place in the puzzle where that tiny piece fit. "Do you think it's the barrier?"

"Maybe." Maya knelt and extinguished the candles one by one, but not in order, and Kiley knew it meant something, the way she did it. She wet her fingertips to check each wick again before she began packing them away with the rest of her ...spell or whatever. "So you couldn't sleep either, huh?"

"No. I thought I'd poke around a little."

"Looking for clues?" Maya asked, glancing up with a hopeful smile.

"Uh-huh."

"Can I come along?"

"Uh-huh."

Maya grinned and rolled up a canvas thingie with all her magic stuff in it, then tucked it into a zipped compartment in her suitcase that was hidden within the lining. Then she put on her cute black ballet slippers and slipped her cellphone into her robe's pocket.

"There's no signal," Kiley reminded her.

"But there is a flashlight app," Maya replied. "And it's easier than carrying one of the big flashlights around."

"Ahh, good thinking."

They headed down the hallway to the curving staircase that spilled down into the foyer, moving soundlessly, Kiley in her spa robe and furry penguin slippers, and Maya in satin and lace. Seemed about right.

In the foyer they stopped and looked around. "Where do we check first?"

Maybe where those lights are, Lady El said.

Kiley said, "What lights?"

And Maya, "What do you mean, what lights?"

Look where you have me pointing, Einstein.

Kiley glanced down, and saw which way her compact mirror was facing. It had slid sideways behind the sash, so she turned to look in that direction, into the depths of the house, where at some far point, there was a window, through which there was a light. Several lights.

"Are those ...*torches*?" Maya asked.

El said, *They'd better not be torches.*

"Probably just tiki torches," Kiley said.

"Not reassuring."

"Let's go out there and see what's going on."

"Dammit, Kiley, I was afraid you were gonna say that."

Tell her about closing the compact!

They crept through the house, exploring none of it. Kiley had hoped to find offices with desk drawers and file cabinets and computers that would tell them exactly what was going on here. And they passed several rooms that might have fit the bill, but they didn't stop. Outside was where the action was, and they both knew it.

Then Maya's phone lit up like a beacon announcing their presence to anyone who might be within range. She pulled it close to her chest, looking down at its face. Then she made an angry sound in her throat. "It's asking if I want to join the Wanderer's Keep Wireless Network," she said.

"There *is* internet out here!"

"Damn straight there is." Maya tapped her phone. "Password protected."

"Of course it is. Fuck." Kiley took a breath, then said, "We know something we didn't before, so that's a plus. Maybe Joe can hack in, or I can, you know, choke the password out of *Julie*."

"Let's keep going," Maya said.

"Fine," Kiley replied. "I can choke Julie later."

They moved further. The hall ended at an open door that led onto a large screened porch. Its floorboards were painted gray, and the screened panes had nothing over them. The two of them could be seen from three sides, if there were anyone around to look. But it was dark. They were shadows amid shadows, so they crouched low, and walked softly, and crossed the wide space to the door at the end that sure as all hell was going to creak when she pushed it open.

They locked eyes. Maya nodded. Kiley pushed the door, then grimaced when its hinges squealed like a politician facing indictment.

She didn't stop pushing though, just shoved through it until the screen door was open far enough that they could both walk through. Then she closed it, and it barely squeaked at all.

"Let's get away from here in case someone heard," Maya whispered, and they followed a path that led away from the house. It skirted widely around the pools and patios where last night's dinner had been served, then bowed back in toward the cliffs on the ocean-facing side of the island.

The path grew steep, and it twisted amid rocks and boulders. The sounds of the waves crashing grew louder the further they went. "I don't see the torches anymore," Kiley said.

"They were this direction, though. I noticed Ursa Minor was right over them and it hasn't been that long." Maya pointed at the sky.

"Of course you did," Kiley said.

Of course she did, Lady El confirmed.

"Look," Maya said as they rounded a large boulder. "Over there."

The lights were back, five of them, in the same pattern as

Maya's candles had been. "What is that, the way they're laid out?"

"Pentacle," Maya said. She pointed at the farthest torch, and drew her finger down to the one on the closest right, then to the middle left, then to the middle right, then the bottom left, and then to the top again, and finally repeated the first line she'd drawn. "Depending on where you start, you can invoke or banish the elements of earth, air, fire, water, and spirit. The one I just drew was to invoke spirit, since we need all the help we can get.

A figure moved past one of the torches, revealing themselves as a shadowy silhouette in a dark, hooded cloak.

They both ducked instinctively, each grabbing the other to pull her down. From behind a pile of boulders, they watched several hooded people moving around in a sandy circle of the beach. They were muttering some kind of incantation and moving their arms in peculiar ways above a small fire in their center.

"What the fuck is going on here?"

JACK DIDN'T SLEEP VERY WELL without Kiley, something she'd hold over his head forever if he admitted it to her. Still ...

When he woke, restless and uneasy, he was in the bed alone. He blinked in the dark bedroom. "Kiley?"

No answer, so he pushed back the covers and slipped out of bed, pulled on some PJ bottoms, and turned on the light. The bathroom door was open and its light was off. Kiley's fluffy penguin slippers were not beside the bed waiting to trip him when he got up in the dark to take a leak, like they usually were.

So he crossed the room and opened the bedroom door, stuck out his head and looked up the hall just in time to see Kiley

going into Maya's room. Ah, okay. Midnight girl talk. That was
fine. Gave him a chance for some private time in Arthur
Kendall's studio. He had a feeling that ghost was the only one
who could tell him what the hell was going on in this place.

He found a T-shirt and those flannel-lined bedroom slippers
Kiley had bought for him. They had hard soles and fake suede
uppers. Then he ducked into the hall and tiptoed past Maya's
room, out to the broad staircase, then down to the landing
where it split. He crossed it and went up into the opposite wing.
He presumed Julie's room was somewhere in this corridor,
which he probably should have thought about sooner. What
would Kiley think if she saw him coming from this wing?

Hell. Well, he'd already made it past all the doors except for
the corner suit that had belonged to Arthur. He might as well
see this through. He went inside, quiet as a mouse, closing the
door behind him, holding his breath, and releasing the knob
slowly, slowly, slowly. The room was empty. Nothing had
changed since he'd been there earlier. But as he went through to
the bottom of the spiral stairway and looked up, he saw light
coming from above.

And there was really no way to climb that metal staircase
quietly. As soon as he lowered his foot onto the second step,
grimacing at the squeaks, a head appeared in the opening above
him. He gasped, then released all his breath at once. "Johnny."

"Looks like we had the same thought," Johnny said, then
looked past him. "Kiley with you?"

"She's in Maya's room. Girl-talk, I guess. You having any luck
up here?"

"So far, no, but I haven't been trying very long." He moved
aside as Jack came the rest of the way up. "Maybe we can try
together."

"Great minds think alike. Let's do this." Jack looked around
the room, past the ugly and impractical wooden cube desk to

the windows beyond. "I see him. He's on the wrap-around deck again, gazing out at something." Jack focused his mind, called out with his heart but with his voice, too. "Arthur. I can see you. I'm here to help."

Arthur immediately faded to nothing.

"Shit."

"What?"

"He vanished."

Nodding, Johnny went to the balcony and opened the sliding door. Jack followed him out into balmy night air. It was heavy and warm, but the breeze made it more refreshing than stifling.

Jack walked out behind him. Johnny turned to face him and said, "My grandfather taught me this. It's a way to induce a receptive state, and I think it'll help me do my thing. Face me, and do as I do." Then he extended his hands up over his head with his palms forward.

Jack raised his own hands up in the same way. Then Johnny pressed their palms together. He said something under his breath, words Jack couldn't make out. But he knew enough to relax his mind, open his senses, and prepare to receive input from sources outside himself—even though he had come to believe that nothing was truly outside himself at all.

His mind stilled. He saw a starry sky, diamonds on velvet. And then, for just an instant, Johnny's hands stopped being there. Jack opened his eyes. Johnny was right there again. He'd been gone—but came back again so fast, he questioned his own perceptions.

Then Johnny opened his eyes and said, "Holy shit."

～

"IT'S A RITUAL," Maya said. "What the hell? Something's happening."

A form took shape in the smoke that rose from the central fire, vaguely human, except for a smoky tail where its legs should be. It had arms, a torso, a head. Its face morphed in and out, the shape changing.

I've never seen anything like that and I've been exploring the occult my whole life, El said.

"Where are the rest of the amulets, Arthur?" The words came from a tall, male figure. He wore a black cloak with a hood so deep you couldn't see his face within its shadows. He was holding something in one outstretched hand, something small enough to fit entirely within his fist. "Tell us."

"Arthur? As in Arthur Kendall?" Kiley whispered.

"Has to be," Maya said. "What does that half-assed witch have in his hand? Wait, is there a chain dangling from it?"

Kiley squinted, leaning closer to get a better look. "I think it *is* a chain. A small one, like a necklace chain."

Talisman. No doubt about it.

"Where are they, Arthur?" The man said, thrusting his fist nearer like a weapon.

The shape in the smoke twisted. A mouth shape opened in the grotesque face, and then there was a moan, an o-shaped sound that might've been the word no, all drawn out in an anguished moan.

"They're hurting him!" Maya sprang up with a rock in her hand and whipped it at the guy holding the chain. It hit his fist dead on. The man yelped, and the thing he'd been holding dropped to the ground.

He turned their way, still holding his injured hand and shouted, "It's the blonde. Get her!" And they all started running toward the rock barricade.

Maya jumped up. "He dropped the chain-thingie. Get it!" Then she ran off in plain sight, knowing damn well they'd all follow.

What the hell did she think was going to happen if they killed her? Shit. Kiley climbed over the rock she'd been hiding behind, and ran to the little fire. On the ground there was a round, gold colored medallion with multiple symbols engraved in its face. She snatched it up and realized by its weight, it wasn't just gold-colored. It was gold. She shoved it onto her robe pocket, and felt it go straight through the hole she'd forgot was there. It hit the ground at her feet, so she grabbed it again and put it around her neck this time. Then she took off after Maya's pursuers.

CHAPTER 9

Johnny wobbled on his feet, caught his balance, and pressed the heel of his hand to his forehead. He'd experienced a rushing sensation in his head, just like that time when he'd been sucked into another person's past—Breia's kid brother Ryan.

He lifted his head and looked around. He was in Arthur Kendall's studio, but it was different. There was light, dancing yellow light, from lit candles on the floor. They surrounded all the hospital bed where Arthur lay.

"It will be just as you always wanted, Arthur," whispered a voice from the shadows beyond the reach of the candle glow.

"The secret to immortality will be known," whispered another.

"Your vision will be fulfilled," said a third.

Johnny could see them as his vision adjusted. They stood in all directions around him, in dark monk's robes with cavernous hoods.

"Not yet," said the man in the bed. His skin bore a gray cast, and his eyes, though dull and bloodshot, were afraid. "There's no body."

"In time, there will be."

"In time for who?"

"All of us."

"I won't last long enough."

"If the barrier works, you will."

One of the forms moved nearer, approaching Arthur's IV pole with a syringe in its gloved hand. The old man lifted his hands from the mattress, but weakly and slowly. He cringed backward into his pillows, and pled, "Not yet. Not yet."

But the person poked the needle straight into the IV bag.

Johnny lunged, but moved straight through them and stumbled forward, expecting to hit the bed, but that wasn't solid either. He finally got his footing and turned to see the plunger already fully depressed. The person was fiddling with the IV's flow control, turning a dial that made soft clicking sounds while the old man reached over and over for the tubing in his arm, missing each time.

Then his fear seemed to leave him all at once as the first drops entered his bloodstream. He breathed a little faster, and then he smiled, started to laugh. He laughed until the laugh turned into a cough.

"Make him stop," Someone hissed.

"He'll be dead in a minute."

"I can't stand it," another voice whispered. They were all soft, those voices—unidentifiable whispers.

One hooded form leaned over the old man. "Let go, Arthur. Die for what you said you believed in all this time. It will give us immortality. It will fulfill your dream."

His coughing eased. His breaths grew weaker as the drug took effect. He rested his head on the pillow, turning his face slightly to one side. He said, "Not without your talismans, it won't."

"What?"

The person leaning over him straightened, then spun around, frantically reversing the dial on the IV. Another came closer and crimped the tube over on itself to stop the flow.

The old man laughed again, three short "Ha" sounds, and the last one ended in a long exhalation. His final breath. One of the hood-wearing people swore and yanked a chain from around Arthur's neck. It had a medal of some kind dangling from it.

Before Johnny could get a closer look at the thing, everything around him blurred and solidified and he was once again standing face-to-face and palm-to-palm with Jack.

"Holy shit," Johnny said.

MAYA RAN for all she was worth back up the path they'd taken from the house. It was steep and twisty, but way too easy for them to follow, so she veered off the path into the rocks and boulders along its steepest side. Loose stones gave way beneath her slippers, and twice she lost her footing and nearly fell. There was nowhere to go from here but straight up, or straight down. And going down would be deadly. Jagged rock outcroppings awaited there like sharp teeth, before giving way to the sandy beach beyond them.

The stony face of the island was steeper and far more dangerous than the path had been. Maya had to climb. The house meant safety. The house meant the rest of the gang, and there was strength in numbers. She wondered if Kiley was okay. Had she got the amulet? Had she made it safely back to the house?

She found a spot between two boulders high on the cliffs above the ocean. She was extra careful where she put her feet as she peered back the way she'd come. Six hooded figures were racing up the path. Behind them, Kiley was coming on strong like a dog chasing a car. What the hell was she going to do when she caught them?

Wait, there had been six hoods. There were only four now. Where were the other two?

"Got you!" Hands clasped Maya's shoulders from behind, startling her so much she sprang up, spun around, and slammed her attacker in the chin with the heel of her hand, just like she'd practiced a hundred times in self-defense class. Only this time, the attacker wasn't in a padded suit and helmet, or standing in a gym on a cushy mat.

His head snapped back, he flew backwards, but he grabbed her shoulders and pulled her down with him. She hit the rocky ground hard, knees first, and yelped in pain. Her attacker sprang to his feet and grabbed her from behind.

"Hey! Get your hands off her!" Kiley shouted.

Maya's relief almost made her weak. Kiley must have seen the struggle and sprinted up here. She slammed into the person —a guy, she was sure, and he stumbled sideways and released Maya. Kiley took Maya's arm and helped her up, but the guy reached for Kiley this time, grabbing at her neck.

"That's enough!" Maya reacted on sheer instinct, slamming both hands into his chest to shove him away from her friend with all she had. He went backwards, right to the edge of the cliff where he teetered, cartwheeling one arm while clinging to Kiley with the other. His upper body was out in space, and the ground was crumbling under his feet. He had hold of Kiley by the chain she wore around her neck. There was no question he was going over the edge, and he might just take Kiley with him.

"Kiley!" Maya caught her by the back of her heavy robe, as the chain snapped and the man fell, screaming.

Kiley teetered and Maya quickly snapped an arm around her waist in the nick of time to pull her back from the brink. It had all happened in a split second, and yet she'd perceived it as if in slow motion.

"Oh, hell. Oh hell, hell, hell." Maya stood there, looking down at where her friend had damn near fallen. The guy who'd grabbed her was down there, his arms and legs bent unnaturally. She watched for a few seconds, waiting for him to move, but he didn't. He just lay there on the shore as frothy waves seemed to reach for him.

Kiley was staring too, until she turned and wrapped her arms around Maya. "You saved my life."

"You'd have done the same for me," Maya said, but her words were muffled by Kiley's thick robe. "Where ...where are the rest of them?"

"They kept going up the path," Kiley replied. "Except for the one who peeled off earlier. Did you see who this guy was?"

"Yeah, just before he fell, his hood dropped. It was the boat pilot, Kevin."

"Son-of-a-gun!" Maya said. "Did you get the talisman?"

"I did." Kiley said slowly. "And I'm damn lucky the chain snapped."

"God." Maya moved Kiley's hair aside and tried to see her neck in the moonlight. There was definitely a mark where the chain had supported the weight of a grown man. "Did you get a look at it?"

"Briefly. I was in kind of a hurry, but I saw that it was a gold medallion with symbols all over it. Do you know what it is?"

"What it is, yes. Not what it does. Not yet. Did you touch it with your bare hands?"

"I did. Was I not supposed to?" Kiley wiped her hands on a flat rock. "If I wasn't supposed to handle it, I wish you'd have said so, Maya."

"We were in a little bit of a hurry," she said. "Just wash your hands and it'll be fine. Sea water would be ideal." She looked down again at the body. "We should search him, see what else he has on him."

"Look, if I need to wash after touching his jewelry, I don't feel so good about touching his body."

But Maya was already making her way down to the shore, knowing Kiley would follow. It took about ten minutes to reach the bottom, meandering between rocks and boulders. Every time she encountered a sheer face, she'd move left or right to find a way to climb around it.

They made their way down with their backs toward the ocean for most of the descent. But Maya could hear the steady rhythm of the waves washing up over the beach, and she was grateful for the sea wind that buffeted her from behind, almost as if it were trying to help her cling to the stone face by pushing her against it.

She finally reached the bottom, and turning, brushed her hands against each other carefully. They were sore from gripping and scraping across stone.

Kiley hopped off a low ledge a few feet to her right and looked back up. "Would've been faster to go back to the path, but at least we got to the bottom in one piece. Where do you think those other hooded goons went?"

"They were headed toward the house. I don't know if they went in or continued into the woods beyond it. I didn't watch that long." Maya looked around the flat, sandy beach where it met the jagged stones at the base of the cliff. But there was no body lying dead upon it.

"Where the hell is boat pilot Kevin?" Kiley asked.

"Maybe he wasn't dead after all," Maya said. "Maybe I didn't really kill him."

"It was self-defense, Maya. It was me-defense, if you want to get specific about it."

"I don't take lives. I don't even swat flies."

"You didn't have a choice."

Maya lowered her head, pinched the bridge of her nose, closed her eyes. "Please let him be alive. Let him be alive."

"SOMEONE'S COMING!" Kiley pointed up at the rocks they'd descended. "*Every*one's coming."

"Thank God," Maya said as the rest of their gang made their way down the path among the rocks.

The two of them stood on the beach where the body had been. Clouds had blotted out the moon, and the wind coming in off the ocean was whipping the palm trees, not to mention their hair.

"Is Joe carrying Breia?" Kiley asked. "Why the hell is Joe carrying Breia?"

"Oh, hell. Kevin *is* dead, isn't he?" Maya shielded her eyes as if that would help her see further in the dark. "She probably got sucked out of her body as soon as he hit the bottom."

"Riiiiiight," Kiley said. "That's gonna take some getting used to." Then she added, "El wants us to make like Nancy Drew and look for clues."

Maya clicked on her flashlight app and resumed skimming the beach where she was sure poor Kevin had wound up. She was shaking and sick to her stomach. She'd taken a life to defend her best friend. It was against everything she believed in and yet she'd do the same again to save Kiley.

"You okay?" Kiley's hand came to her shoulder.

She nodded, because she wasn't ready to talk about it. "He was right there, near as I can estimate." She pointed at a spot on the beach, where the waves chased each other over the sand, then hissed as they backed away again. "I don't even see the imprint he must've made when he landed."

"But we're sure he was dead, right? Breia is probably proof, if we still need it."

Maya nodded, turning toward the cliffs again as the horror replayed in her mind. "He hit that big pear-shaped boulder so hard, he ricocheted all the way to the surf." She aimed her light at the rock, then said, "Oh, yeah, there's blood." And her stomach heaved. She lowered her head to hide it.

Jack hit the bottom first, ran right to Kiley and wrapped her up in his arms. And then Johnny did exactly the same to Maya, and she knew she should object, but she didn't. He hugged her up close to him and rocked side to side and ran a hand over her hair and down her back over and over.

It felt so freaking good having his arms around her. She pressed closer. He cupped the back of her head and bent his, and for a second, she was sure they were going to kiss. But then she lowered her chin just slightly, and he read the signal and backed up a little.

When he raised his head again, he said, "Breia said someone on the island had died. She made us bring her outside the house, so she could get to them. You know, in death fairy form."

"We were terrified for you," Jack put in. He, too, had pulled back a little and was gazing at Kiley's face. Closer to the rocks, Joe stood awkwardly, holding Breia in his arms like a sleeping princess he'd just rescued from a tower.

"Somebody *did* die," Kiley said. "Kevin, the boat pilot."

"I killed him." Maya looked Johnny in the eyes when she said it.

"You did not kill him," Kiley said. "He attacked us both and you defended us. You didn't mean for him to go over the edge, but you kept him from taking me with him."

"I didn't mean for him to go over, either. But I did it. I took a life. He's dead because of me."

"He's dead because of him," Johnny said, and he pushed her

hair off her face and tucked it behind her ear. "Maybe you'd better tell us what happened."

Maya nodded.

Joe looked around and found a dry patch of beach surrounded by smaller boulders, far enough from shore that the tide wouldn't reach her there. He laid Breia down in the sand.

Maya walked over there and knelt beside Joe to check on her.

"She passed out the second we left the house," Joe said. "I'm just glad it didn't happen on the cliffs."

Kiley sat down on a boulder beside Jack. "It's dangerous, isn't it? This thing of hers. It could happen when she's driving, swimming, I don't even know what all."

Joe nodded. "She shouldn't be doing any of those things alone. You just never know when it could happen."

"I don't like that we can't see her right now," Maya said. "The other her, I mean."

"The winged-one," Kiley said.

"What if she gets into trouble?" Maya asked. "If we can see her, and the dead people can see her, then those cultists are going to see her, and then what will they do?"

"Cultists?" Jack looked at Maya, then at Kiley beside him. "There are cultists?"

"There are cultists," Kiley said.

"I saw them too, when I blipped out in the studio," Johnny said. "Breia come looking for us before I could relay any of that."

Jack was looking from one face to the next. "Please explain."

Maya didn't say anything, and Kiley seemed to read that. She spoke instead. "Neither of us could sleep so we decided to do a little snooping," she said. "We saw lights, torches as it turns out, in a clearing back that way." She pointed back into the woods to the north. "So we snuck down to see what was going on."

"It was a ritual," Maya said, her voice shaky. "There were six people. They wore dark colored robes with deep hoods, so we couldn't see their faces. They pulled in Arthur's spirit, that poor man."

"So that's where he went," Jack said softly, with a quick look Johnny's way.

"They kept demanding to know where the rest of the talismans were," Kiley said.

"That matches what I saw," Johnny said. "I blipped back in time to Arthur's death. A bunch of people in monk's robes injected something into his IV. It killed him. They were talking about his dream, about achieving immortality for all of them, like it was part of some plan. But apparently he had to die to get it underway and the others were tired of waiting."

"My God!" Maya said. "Arthur was murdered?"

Johnny nodded. "Just before he died, he said they couldn't do whatever it was they were planning without their talismans. Apparently he'd hidden them."

Maya closed her hand around Johnny's bicep. "When they conjured him in the fire just now, they were asking him where he'd hidden the talismans. They had one, but there must be others."

"And they dropped the one they had," Kiley said. "I had it for a second, but then Kevin took it over the edge and almost me, too."

Jack swore softly and put his arms around her. "I only got a brief look at it," Kiley went on. "It was heavy. Gold, I think. And there were initials, an A and a K kind of squished together, and a bunch of other symbols around the outer edge."

"A.K. for Arthur Kendall," Joe said slowly. He'd risen from Breia's side and come to the stones that surrounded her where the others had sort of gathered.

Johnny said, "So something, probably the barrier, is keeping his ghost trapped here and other non-physical beings from passing in or out of the house."

"But this *is* out of the house," Joe said. "They summoned him out here, you said."

"They control him." Maya nodded, thinking it through. "With the talisman, Maybe. That would be my guess."

"So maybe when we find it again, we smash it to bits against one of these boulders," Jack suggested.

"I don't think it's smashable," Maya said. "It will have to be ritually deactivated and returned to the earth. But before we can do any of that, we have to find it again."

"We've gotta find Breia first," Joe said. "I don't like this." He took off his robe, which he'd worn over pajamas and laid it over Breia's physical form. "We should get her back inside. It's chilly out here."

"Not until she's back in her body," Kiley said. "Remember what happened last time. She couldn't get back in."

"All the more reason to find her," Maya said. "And when we do, I bet we'll find Kevin's body, too."

"And whoever *moved* Kevin's body," Kiley added. "And maybe the pretty gold necklace too. I really wish I'd dressed for this."

CHAPTER 10

K iley and Jack went back to the house for supplies; flashlights clothing, shoes, jackets. Jack gathered up stuff for the guys, and Kiley hit Maya and Breia's rooms to gather some of their things for them, and her own to get dressed.

Her fuzzy penguin slippers had served her well. She'd forgot she even had them on her feet when she'd seen Maya locked in mortal combat with one of those hooded jerks on the cliffs.

Thanks, Kiley, Lady El said. Kiley had set the compact on the night stand while she pulled on capris-length jeans, a baby tee, and a denim jacket.

"For what?"

You closed the compact. You were being pulled inexorably over a cliff and you took the time to reach down and close the compact. I'll never forget it as long as I ...well, you know.

"I didn't know what would happen if the glass got smashed on the way down," Kiley said. "Besides, I promised."

She picked up the golden clamshell and tucked it into her jeans pocket, still opened, and as she did, she realized she was friends, good friends, with a dead jazz singer from the sixties. And it didn't even seem all that weird.

She met Jack in the hallway. "Did you check on Julie?"

He nodded. "Yeah, just like you asked. I found her room in the west wing, closest one to Arthur's, opened the door real quiet, and she was sound asleep in her bed inside."

"Huh." Kiley mulled on that. "Could she have been faking? Fully dressed under the covers, maybe in a monk's robe?"

"I didn't check. But it didn't seem that way to me." At her frown he shrugged and said, "Anything's possible, though."

Together, they started back down the stairs. He said, "I don't have a great feeling about this."

"We'll be fine," she told him. "We're always fine."

"I know, but this feels different."

Kiley met his eyes and nodded. "It does, doesn't it?"

"I want you to know I love you," he said. "And only you. And my biggest regret right now is not telling you about my past."

"I know."

"Do you, though? Do you really?"

She stood there in the hallway, just before the downward staircase, and looked at his face. She loved his face, so it wasn't really fair, but she looked at it anyway.

This is a good man, Lady El said from her pocket.

"I know he's a good man, El."

Jack frowned at her.

You wouldn't want to live without him.

"No, I wouldn't want to live without him," Kiley said.

Jack caught on, glanced down at the compact mirror sticking out of her jeans' pocket, and winked.

Back atcha, sexy.

"Down, girl."

Well, if you're not going to forgive him—

"I forgive him!" she blurted. She shoved the compact deeper into her pocket, and said, "I forgive you, Jack. I do. I forgive you.

I'm gonna do my best to let this go and move past it. And I love you, too."

He pulled her closer to seal that with a kiss.

Let me out of here! Lady El affected a muffled voice, and probably thought she was hilarious.

But Kiley was too busy getting kissed to be bothered by it.

They took the back staircase that emerged in the kitchen, and headed out the back door from there, because it was closer.

"I DON'T LIKE the looks of that sky," Joe said.

He was sitting on a rock on Maya's left. Johnny sat on another rock to her right. Maya was in the middle, staring out at the ocean, and feeling awful. She didn't want to be near either of them right then, so she rose and walked toward the water, then stood, gazing out at it.

Every death is a suicide. Those wise words had been given to her by one of her earliest spiritual teachers, a woman who'd called herself Silver in honor of the moon. When it is time, she had said, the soul finds the path of least resistance much like lightning does. It zigs this way and that way, touching each component needed to end the physical life and break the body's hold on the soul, allowing it to transition out of the physical realm and rejoin the bigger part of itself, which was the sum total of every lifetime every lived by that being. And so much more.

Was she one of the components needed for Kevin to make his exit? She must've been the main one. And yet she didn't feel like a piece of nature's puzzle. She felt like a killer.

She could hear the guys chatting behind her. Their voices were a low murmur and then suddenly they got louder in a way that made her turn to see what was going on.

Johnny and Joe were standing facing each other in front of the boulders that surrounded Breia's temporary bed. Maya started toward them and heard Johnny say, "Maybe you should give a little more thought to how you're making Maya feel."

"Maybe *you* should!" Joe countered, which was meaningless. But Joe wasn't great at snappy comebacks. He was a deliberate man. He usually thought before he spoke.

"Maybe Maya can speak for herself," she said, heading closer to them. "Knock it off, right now."

"No," Johnny said. "Look, it's not okay, him falling all over Breia right in front of you—"

"Johnny stop."

"It's disrespectful, and honest to God, so unlike you to put up with it!"

"I'm not dating Joe!" She blurted it just like that. Didn't plan it, didn't work her way up to it, didn't ease into it. Just blurted it.

Johnny stood there staring at her. They were between the little circle of boulders, and the water's edge, the three of them standing close to each other.

"What do you mean?" Johnny asked. "You saying you two broke up?"

She lowered her head and sighed.

"We were never together," Joe said. "Well, we were, years ago, but not this time."

Johnny frowned at him, and the frown turned to a scowl and he faced Maya again. "What is he talking about?"

She took a deep breath, lifted her chin, looked him in the eyes. Joe turned, and walked a few steps away, toward the beach, giving them a moment.

"Well?"

"I asked Joe to pretend we were seeing each other."

"To keep me away from you?"

"To give you an easy out," she said. "Johnny, I'm too old for you."

"That's bullshit and you know it."

"I thought if I backed off you and Breia could—"

"Breia and I are friends. We've never *been* anything but friends and we'll never *be* anything but friends." He lowered his head. "I thought you wanted to be my friend, too, Maya. But friends don't lie to each other like this."

"I know."

"I can't believe ..." He looked down the beach at Joe, then back at her. Joe had reached the water, kicked a seashell like he was angry at it, then turned and started back toward the circle of rocks where Breia was lying.

"This was low, Maya. It was beneath you."

"I know. I'm sorry." She also knew her apology wasn't enough to make things right, but for the life of her, she didn't know what would be.

"Are you?"

"Yes. And just so you know, Joe said if I didn't tell you the truth, he would. And now he's kind of here, and you two hate each other and it's because of my lie, and I need to fix this. I need you to let me fix this."

"I don't know that there's any way to fix it," Johnny said.

Kiley and Jack came out of the rocks and over to where they were. Jack handed Johnny some clothes, and Johnny went a few steps away and dressed in the shelter of giant fern. Joe took his and went the opposite way.

Kiley handed clothes to Maya, and she moved behind a tree to put them on and watched her friend head toward Breia with a jacket for her. But she stopped and turned back and called out, "Where's Breia?"

"What do you mean, where's Breia?" She's right there." Joe moved around the rocks, and Maya came out from behind her tree and headed there, too, but Breia was not lying in the sand where she had been.

"She must've come back to her body and ..." Maya shook her head. "Got up and walked away? That doesn't make any sense."

"There are footprints," Jack said. "Not hers, and not here, further out from the rocks, but still." He knelt in the sand. "They go this way. Come on."

"You think somebody *took* her?" Maya looked around at her friends. "Is that what this is, somebody took her?" When her questing gaze landed on Johnny's, he looked away. He was angry. She had hurt him. She had to find a way to make him understand that she'd only been trying to do what was best for him.

"No more sand," Jack said. "No more prints."

"Follow the trajectory, though," Kiley said.

"The trajectory leads to a stone wall." Jack walked right up to the sheer rock face. It was layered in vines and moss, and he brushed them away, then went quiet. "Wait. This ...doesn't feel solid." He pushed on the rock and said, "It gives. This isn't right, this is ..."

Johnny ran up beside him and started running his hands over the face of the stone. Jack was doing the same, pushing away vines, scrubbing off moss.

"There's a seam." Johnny ran his hands over the edge of the stone, where a very straight crack separated it from the rest of the wall. He had great hands, strong and elegant at the same time. Maya had always loved his hands.

"No way that's natural," Kiley said.

"There's one on my side too." Jack followed it upward, and then across the top. "How the hell does it—?"

"Got it," Johnny did something and the stone rolled inward as smoothly as if it were on wheels. No noise. It backed up enough to leave a gap they could walk through.

Maya moved up closer as several of them aimed their flashlights into the cave. Joe came with her, really close to her side. "Sorry I messed things up."

"I messed things up," she said.

Johnny was the first one to go in through the opening. Jack and Kiley were behind him.

"His feelings are hurt," Joe said. "If he knew the truth, they wouldn't be. I mean, that's how I'd feel."

"What's how you'd feel?" She asked, whispering the words and worrying because Johnny was getting so far ahead of them. Jack and Kiley, too, of course.

Joe shrugged his shoulders, an exaggerated motion due to his long, tall frame. He was handsome in a gangly, nerdy sort of way. She'd always appreciated intelligence in a man, and Joe had more of it than anyone she'd ever met.

"Tell me," she said. "Tell me the truth, I need to hear it. What did you mean? How would you be feeling?"

Joe sighed heavily as they moved deeper into the cave. "I'm no authority on romance, that's for sure, so this is pure conjecture. But I suspect I'd feel as if ..." He hesitated, and she gave him a head-bob with bug-eyes to prod him on. "... as if you not only didn't want to be with me, but wanted to not be with me so bad you made up a whole other relationship just to get rid of me."

"Oh, hell, really?"

"Sorry. You said you wanted the truth."

"So how do I fix this?"

He held up both hands. "Again, not my specialty. But maybe next time bounce your ideas off me *before* you execute?"

"I might just do that," she said. She trusted Joe. She trusted him as she had few people in her entire life. "I'm glad we're still friends. You know that, right?"

"I'm glad, too." Then he picked up his pace, and moved deeper into the dark cave.

Maya followed, glad to have a flashlight instead of just her phone to light her way. She hadn't gone far, when she heard something behind her and spun around to see the stone sliding back into place. They were sealed in.

~

KILEY and the others all turned when the giant slab of rock slid itself back into place.

Ohhhhh, I don't like this one little bit, Lady El said.

"You want me to close the compact and send you home?" Kiley pulled the mirror out of her pocket and looked at Lady El. She wore a turban, green with hot pink and yellow flowers. The pink paper umbrella from a tropical drink was stuck into its folds. Her eyes were wide.

Not just yet, she said. *I think my curiosity outweighs my fear. Just remember your promise.*

"I swear, Lady El, I'll close the compact before I die."

Everybody looked at her, having heard only her side of the conversation. "What? She doesn't want to be stuck in the compact watching our corpses rot."

"Jeeze, Kiley," Maya rubbed her arms as if they had goosebumps.

"Come on, let's go find our death fairy."

At this point, the cave was only wide enough for them to walk two-abreast. Jack picked up his pace to catch Kiley, Johnny was right behind them, walking alone. Kiley had noticed him not looking at or talking to Maya and wondered what the hell had happened while she and Jack were gathering supplies.

"Jack checked Julie's bedroom," she said, aiming her flashlight ahead. "He thinks she was in it."

"She was in it. Sound asleep—"

"Or faking being sound asleep and wearing a monk's robe under the blankets."

"There have to be a dozen people on her staff, though," Maya said. "Maybe twenty. There were only six in the grove, you said."

"Still ..." Kiley looked at Jack. "I kind of wish you'd stomped right in there and started yanking off covers."

"Yeah, I'm not that guy," he said.

She was glad he was not that guy and felt a little soft and mushy when he said it. She'd forgiven him for not telling her about being married for a dozen weeks in his teens. She'd weighed the options and decided she'd prefer having what they had together, to holding onto her indignation, no matter how righteous.

What in the name of Billie Holiday is that? Lady El was back in Kiley's jeans' pocket, facing forward.

An odd blue glow was coming from further in, and Kiley held a hand out to one side, palm backward, and stopped moving.

Everybody else stopped moving, too.

"We need to be silent from here," she whispered, glancing behind her. Johnny nodded. So did Maya and Joe. "Stay near the walls, keep low. We don't know what's up there."

They crept closer. Kiley couldn't have stepped with more care if she'd been walking over unicorn eggs. And she couldn't have walked closer to Jack's side unless she rode along in his pocket.

The cave widened into a large section, roughly circular, and rising much higher than the passage. But the most noticeable thing was the nude body in the center. Kevin. His skull was caved in on one side, but someone had stripped him and washed away the blood that must have been there. His arms and legs had been laid out straight, but you could still see the places where the bones no longer met. An elbow had moved around to the side of his arm, his shin jogged sharply to the left halfway down, and his head was no longer centered atop his neck.

His flesh was white, and a weird blue glow surrounded him.

"We must be directly beneath the house," Joe whispered.

"I don't see anyone else down here," Maya added.

"I do," Jack said.

They all looked at him, and he nodded toward the dead man. "Kevin. His ghost, anyway. He's trapped near the body. He can't get out." He held up a hand. "Hey, Kev. We're here to help."

Maya said, "I'm so sorry, Kevin. I didn't mean to hurt you." Then she turned in a slow circle, looking around the edges of the wide chamber. "Look," she said, pointing.

For the first time Kiley saw the items on the floor, forming a gigantic ring around the body that nearly filled the entire chamber. They were stones, fist-sized, unevenly shaped, with jagged edges. And they were glowing. They formed the boundary of that eerie blue luminescence.

"What kind of rocks are those?" Kiley asked. "Deep, iridescent blues and greens like that?"

"Similar to labradorite," Maya said.

"Yes, but I don't think labradorite glows." Joe took off his glasses, wiped the lenses with his shirt and put them back on. "You know, as a rule."

"That would be the magic," Maya whispered. "You guys watch my back." She started toward the nearest wall, moving past Johnny, past Kiley and Jack.

Kiley stepped out behind her, and moved left, while Jack moved right, walking the permeter of the blue glow. There were stone walls, stalactites pointed down from above as if threatening.

Maya was kneeling beside the closest stone. Johnny had entered the room and moved up to stand behind her. Kiley thought that whatever had happened between them, he'd set it aside for the moment. Joe lingered in the doorway, as if unsure what to do.

Maya pressed her palms together in a sort of salutation, then she pressed them to the ground and spoke in that special tone she only used for magic. It was deeper, smoother, and the vowel sounds were elongated and almost musical.

"Earth around me, Earth below me, Earth above me, Earth within me, Earth my body, Earth my mother, Earth my source, Earth my power."

Then she reached out for the glowing stone, closed her hand around it, and pulled it toward her.

It glowed brighter, and she hissed as if it burned, dropped it, and fell backward, holding one hand with the other. The stone snapped back into place as if had been attached by a rubber band.

Johnny was on his knees beside her before the rock touched down, taking her wrist and looking into her palm. "There's no mark," he said.

"Well, there should be!" She pulled her hand free and blew on it. "Burns like a brand!"

Jack moved closer to the barrier, but didn't touch anything. He said, "Kevin, we're going to find a way to free you, okay? Just stay calm. We need time to figure out what's going on so we can help you. But I promise you, we will."

Then he tipped his head to one side as if listening.

"What?" Kiley asked. "What's he saying?"

"He wants to show us something," Jack said. "He wants to show *you*, Johnny."

"How does he know he *can* show me?"

"We know things when we're dead," Maya told him. She put a hand on his shoulder. "Our disbelief stays behind with our bodies. Our misguided notions. Our mistakes and limitations. Our bad feelings and hurt and pride. They all stay behind and stop blocking out the truth. At least, for most of us." She took his hand in hers, and he shot her a look of surprise. "Be careful. Keep hold of my hand to stay grounded. We don't need anyone else getting stuck outside their bodies.

MAYA CLUNG to Johnny's hand as they moved together into the blue glow. "I suspect this is the energy barrier," she said. "It extends all the way up through the entire house. We can't take it down without removing those stones. I mean, it would take a power stronger than mine to do it, at least."

He met her eyes and nodded once. There was hurt in his eyes, and he couldn't hold hers for more than a few seconds at a time.

He seemed to shake his feelings off, then he knelt down, reached out, put his hand on the dead man's shoulder.

Suddenly the glow around the ghost and its dearly departed body, got brighter, then solidified into a solid blue sphere, backlit like an old-fashioned computer screen. It darkened to black and a scene played out before Maya's eyes. She realized that she was seeing what Johnny was seeing.

There were five cloaked figures dragging Kevin's body along the passage and into the cave. Kevin's body, only he was not dead —not quite.

Maya heard a gurgling sound, what some might call a death rattle. The people dragging him stopped, and one of them bent close, then knelt and pumped Kevin's heart insistently, until it had regained a weak, stuttering beat. She could hear the heart-beat somehow. Maybe because Johnny was hearing it, and maybe he was hearing it because Kevin had heard it himself. It seemed like torture that they wouldn't let him die.

They resumed pulling him by his arms until they were in the

wide, circular chamber, and dragged him all the way into the center of its glowing blue light. Then one bent to press an ear to Kevin's chest.

Maya could hear what that person was hearing. Two weak percussions of Kevin's heart. Then a long pause. Then a soft, stuttering beat. Then another long pause. As the robed figure listened, the beat came less and less frequently, and soon, it came not at all.

Then that figure straightened and nodded and the others gathered to stand around Kevin's body, silent and watching. One of them draped a talisman around his neck and tucked it inside his shirt, and they all began chanting something in a forgotten language.

They were interrupted when a streak of light came flying out of the cave wall toward the group in the center. The light hit the blue glow and bounced off it as if it were solid, landing on the floor as it solidified into Breia. She sat there, stunned, shook her head, then blinked and took in her surroundings. The hooded figures whirled toward her, shouting and cursing. Maya couldn't hear them. If was as if someone had hit the mute button.

Breia got up slowly, looking at them, her eyes wide. Their faces were hidden in the depths of their hoods, which gave even Maya a case of the creeps and would scare the daylights out of Breia. She took a step backwards, and her wings extended all at once, wide and beautiful, as white as purity itself.

One of the hooded figures lunged at her and she seemed to fade. Suddenly you could see right through her, and the attacker's hand went right through her, too. And then Breia vanished, just disappeared entirely. Maya thought she was still there, but had become invisible.

Finally, Johnny thought, or maybe he said it, if you could call it that in whatever state he was in, whatever state Maya was currently witnessing through his senses. *I've been telling her for weeks that there had to be a way for her to go unseen. Because she can't be the only one, and if there are others, and they're all visible to the living, then their existence would be common knowledge by now.*

"That makes sense," Maya said, or maybe she only thought it. She was kind of lost in Johnny's experience.

I don't think she's supposed to be visible to anyone other than the soul she's helping, he told her. *She said she'd tried, but had no idea if it had worked. How would she know, if there were no living people around to witness it?*

An instant after Breia vanished, the same beam of light she had been on arrival flashed once and then exited straight through the cave's stone wall.

The cloak-wearing asshats fled through a tunnel at the opposite end of the chamber from the one through which the gang had entered. The passage was narrower, and there were crystals that gleamed from its walls, and a stone stairway leading upward, cut into the rock on one side.

No time to explore that now. Still clinging to her hand, Johnny followed the cultists through the tunnel, and somehow never fell behind the running, robed figures. Then one of them, tripped and fell into a stone protrusion that stuck out further than it should. That monk-robe-wearing villain pressed gloved hands to the outcropping, and it moved a little. So they kept moving it, first one way and then another, until the large rock came loose, and fell to the floor. There was a dark chasm in the stone where the rock had been. The hooded reached in and pulled something out. A black drawstring bag.

They untied the knot and loosened the strings, revealing a purple lining. Inside, gold gleamed. A tangle of chains and golden talismans lay in the bottom of the bag.

Maya felt an unbearable sensation of being sucked out of existence and knew it was what Johnny was feeling. His hand tightened around hers.

And then it was over. He opened his eyes, and so did Maya. She found herself kneeling beside Johnny, who still had one hand on Kevin's body, and one hand wrapped around hers.

Maya knew that to their friends, he'd blipped out and back faster then the flash of a strobe light. "They found the rest of the talismans," Maya said. "They have what they need to do whatever evil they're up to."

"You saw it too?" Johnny asked in what sounded like wonder.

Maya nodded. "I think I went with you."

He held her eyes for a split second, then released her hand and got to his feet. "Breia was here," he said. "They saw and went after her. We have to find her before they do." He looked at the body on the floor. "He's not going anywhere."

"His spirit's trapped in that barrier, just like Arthur's up in the house," Jack said with a sad look at the empty space around the body.

"Let's go find Breia," Joe said. And he didn't even wait, but started back through the tunnel to the cave's entrance. Jack and Kiley followed, leaving Johnny and Maya to bring up the rear.

But as they walked away, an icy tingle tiptoed up Maya's spine, that feeling like someone is standing behind you, watching you, and when she turned, she could've sworn that dead Kevin's hand was in a different position than it had been before.

"Come on, Maya! We have to hurry."

"I think his hand moved."

Johnny looked behind them, but Kevin's corpse lay still and broken. "That's even more reason to hurry."

CHAPTER 11

They headed back to the place where they'd left Breia's body, working under the assumption that she had returned to it and taken off running, knowing the cultists were in hot pursuit. She must have been so panicked, Maya thought, that she hadn't even noticed her friends a few yards further down the beach.

Maya pointed at the spot where the woods were most dense. "If I were fleeing from hooded goons, I'd have gone that way," she said.

"That would make sense," Johnny agreed. "And she won't go far. She's usually pretty wiped out after one of these excursions."

Maya met his eyes, but he quickly averted them and started off into the trees. She'd thought they'd had a moment, back there in the cave, holding hands while he blipped into the past to witness what had happened.

Thick trees, flowering dogwood, wild olive, red by, and other trees Maya couldn't name, rose from thick beds of waist-high ferns and undergrowth. She tried to focused on Breia, feeling for her energy as they all trudged deeper into the woods

Joe was moving faster and had pulled ahead of the others. He kept whisper shouting her name.

"I wonder what made Kevin change sides?" Johnny asked.

"Well, it's like I said, we lose a lot of our flawed notions when we die. According to what I've read, we kind of leave all that baggage behind with our bodies."

"I don't think that's always true, though. Breia's parents certainly didn't."

Maya shrugged. "Maybe it's a choice. Maybe with some it takes longer to shed the old beliefs. Maybe it's something else entirely. I don't think we'll know until we cross over ourselves."

He nodded, looked at her, looked away.

"I didn't mean to hurt you, you know," she said. There was enough distance between them and the others for privacy. Jack and Kiley had veered left to cover a wider swath of woods and Joe was yards ahead by now.

"You think you know what's best for me better than I do. It's not only hurtful, Maya, it's insulting."

She lowered her head. "I'm sorry."

He heaved a sigh, then said, "She got farther than I thought. Poor kid, must be wiped out."

He'd shifted the subject away from them, which was wise. They should be focused on Breia and she knew it. And it seemed she'd done serious damage to her relationship with Johnny. It would take more than a conversation to fix it. And she didn't know where to begin.

Ahead of them, Joe came to a sudden halt and lifted one hand to signal them to stop as well. Then he started forward again, but slowly. As they caught up to him, Maya saw the way he placed each foot with care, stepping as silently as he could, and she immediately did the same.

And then she saw the small form ducked between a fern and a thick tree root that arched up from the ground.

Joe took one more step, then said, "Breia!"

"Joe!" She sprang upright, ran and smashed herself against him. "Thank goodness! They were chasing me."

"We know—"

"And there was a dead man—"

"Kevin, the boat pilot. We know."

"And it was just like with Arthur. There was some kind of barrier that kept his soul trapped inside. I couldn't get into it and he couldn't get out."

"We know," Joe repeated.

"We?" She finally uncurled her arms from around him long enough to look past him, where Maya and the others had all closed ranks. "Oh." She took another step backward. "Sorry, Maya."

"It's okay," Joe said. "Everybody knows Maya and I aren't really together."

"They do?" she asked.

"We do?" Kiley repeated.

"*She* knew?" Maya said

"Look, let's get back to the house. I think it's the safest place for us right now," Jack said.

"Safe?" Maya asked. "What's safe there? For all we know, Julie and her staff are those hooded goons."

Johnny said, "I think we should follow that other tunnel and that upward passage out of the cave to see where they lead."

"Not tonight, my friend," Jack said. "Not when we know a bunch of hooded maniacs are stealing bodies and chasing women through the jungle."

"It's not precisely a jungle," Joe said, "But I concur. The house is safer than the woods."

"Everyone else?" Kiley asked.

"I don't really care where their secret tunnels lead," Maya said. "I just want off this island."

"Me, too." Breia nodded. Everyone kept touching her, hugging her, reassuring her. She should've known her friends wouldn't let her flee demons on her own. "But until we find the boats—"

"Okay, fine, you're right. Our top goals are to find a way off this island and get to safety," Johnny said.

Joe agreed and Jack said, "And since we can't search for the boats with a bunch of maniacs running around the woods, let's at least wait for daylight. Until then, I still think we have to hole up in the house."

"Me, too, I guess," Maya said, looking around.

Breia nodded, then widened her eyes and said, "But *not* in separate rooms! We should all stay together. There's safety in numbers, right?"

THEY TREKKED FOREVER through mosquito-infested woods, until Kiley spotted what looked like a road in the early morning light, and followed it back to the mansion. Just coming around the bend into sight of it knocked the wind out of her. The place was stunning by night, lit by ground-level lights that shone up on it like they were highlighting a masterpiece in a museum. It was a crying shame it was inhabited by crazies.

Julie being the chief nut job of them all. Because, sound asleep in her bed or not, she was the queen of this freaking island, and anything that happened here, happened on her watch.

They went around back, to try to enter the way they'd exited, through that discreet kitchen door. Kiley tiptoed up to it, and had opened it partway before she realized there were people inside.

Beasley, the cook, spread melted butter and cinnamon onto a

rolled-out square of dough, then rolled it up, and proceeded to slice it. Each slice went onto a baking sheet.

"Don't stand there holding the door open!" she said, looking their way. "The bugs!"

"Sorry." Kiley shouldered her way inside, looking around the room. There were four people there. The cook and three others she'd seen around the place, including the one who'd shown them how to find the dinner party and the one who'd helped served the meal.

She measured them up for their monk-robe sizes. Beasley was working on the fruit, washing it all, peeling the oranges. A scrawny red-haired kid with abundant freckles ran around picking up after them, gathering every scrap, washing off every used surface, cleaning every dish or utensil the second it was put down.

She moved into the kitchen, and the others followed single-file, toward the stairway door. "We were out early, exploring and um, didn't want to wake Julie."

"You could scream at the top of your lungs from your wing, and she wouldn't hear you in hers," the cook said. "No one would."

Well that wasn't creepy at all, Lady El said from Kiley's jeans' pocket.

"Do you all live here in the house?" Jack asked. Kiley had already reached the stair door, pulled it open and held it as Joe and Breia moved past her and up.

"Nah, we have our own cabins," Freckles said. "windward side of the island."

"Cool," Jack said. "You have your own boats too?"

"Well, we—"

"These pots aren't going to clean themselves, Bruno," the cook interrupted.

Bruno? Seriously? Lady El rolled her eyes. *He does not look like a Bruno.*

"I know, right?" Kiley muttered.

Maya and Johnny were heading past her up the stairs, keeping watch behind Breia.

"Well, I guess we'll see you at breakfast then."

"Not unless you're dining with the staff," Cook said. "This is a staff entrance. That's a staff stairway. Use the ones that aren't."

"Nobody told us," Jack said.

She sniffed in fake indignation. "Some things ought to be obvious."

"Screw you," said Kiley, "and the black hooded cloak you rode in on." Then she shoved Jack ahead of her and slammed the stair door behind her while the cook gaped.

As they hurried along the corridor toward their rooms, Kiley said, "Wait!" and everyone skidded to a halt. "We agreed to stay together from now on, yes?" Everyone nodded. "So whatever each of you need from your room, let's get it now, one room at a time, all of us together. Maya's room is first."

"I'm so glad she's our leader," Breia whispered to Joe.

"I thought Jack was the leader," he replied.

So, room by room, they did what needed doing. The six of them trooped in, helped pack up, and moved on. Without prior consultation, each person seems to be packing everything they'd brought with them right back into the luggage in which they'd brought it.

Jack and Kiley's suite was last, and by the time they got there, the rest of the gang were dragging suitcases and duffels behind them.

They all went in, Kiley closed and locked the door, and then everyone sort of stood around looking at her, like soldiers awaiting their orders.

"Anybody going to be able to sleep?" she asked.

Breia raised her hand, but nobody else did. Almost apologetically, she said, "It takes a lot out of me, popping in and out of my body."

"Not to mention running a half marathon with crazy people on your tail," Maya said.

"Popping in and out exhausts me, too," Johnny said. "I think I could probably rest a little."

"What do you mean, Johnny?" Breia was the only one unaware of what had happened in the cave. "You popped out?"

"Yeah I popped back in time to see what happened in the cave. I saw them drag Kevin's body in there. His heart stopped, I think more than once on the way, but they resuscitated him. Then I saw you come in. Saw those assholes chasing you out of the cave. On the way, one of them found the missing talismans."

"Now that I think about it," Kiley said, "that's probably the jewelry we were hired to find."

"Wow. You think?" Breia asked.

But Maya still seemed stuck on Johnny being wiped out by his gift. "I didn't know it tired you when you did that, Johnny," she said. "Does it have any other side effects?"

He shrugged. "Too soon to tell, I guess."

Brrr, you feel that chill in here? He is icy toward our girl.

"You got that right." Nobody even looked at Kiley strangely anymore when she talked to her invisible friend.

"What do we have for weapons?" Johnny asked. Yeah, he was in a fighting mood, and Kiley was glad because she was ready to kick some ass herself.

Jack pumped his hands in a slow-down motion. "I think we need to run through this thing first. If nothing else, it'll help us process what we know and maybe decompress a little. So, what have we learned tonight?"

Breia raised her hand as if she were a school kid, but started talking before anyone called on her. "I think I'm not supposed to be visible when I go to help the dead," Breia said. "It's just like Johnny's been telling me. But then I'd just be a voice in the darkness."

"We learn through experimentation," Joe said. "Try it next time. At least, next time there's a soul you can get to."

"What is up with that, anyway?" Maya asked. "They've got Arthur trapped in the house, and now poor Kevin in the cave below. What use is there for captive ghosts?"

"Gotta be about power," Jack said. "With humans it's always money, sex, or power."

"Well, that's a sunny attitude," Kiley said.

"It's not an attitude, it's a fact."

"What about love?" Maya looked from Jack to Johnny. "Sometimes it has to be about love."

"That falls under sex," Jack replied.

"In the patriarchy, maybe." She tossed her hair.

"We're all stressed." Breia said it so softly it was like she didn't want anyone to hear her.

"Let's go over what we know," Kiley sat on a chair, and everyone else found a place to perch, too, following her lead. There was a basket of fruit on the coffee table, so she dug through the apples, bananas and strawberries, and found a sleeve of Oreos underneath. "Score. Twelve in a sleeve, that's two apiece." She opened them up and passed the sleeve around.

Breia looked around until she found a pad and pen, then returned to her spot next to Joe on the sofa. Johnny and Maya were about as far apart as they could be, her in a chair, him on an antique trunk that stood in the corner.

"Okay, we know there are at least four people who saw Breia's secret identity as the death fairy," Kiley said. "Five if you count dead Kevin. And We know these same people trapped Kevin the boat pilot's soul in that cave. We can surmise the same gang probably trapped Arthur in the house, because, how many people go around doing that, really?"

"Plus, I saw them kill him," Johnny said. "They mentioned needing to test the barrier"

Kiley ate a cookie, looking around the room to see the others nodding.

"What if they want to do the same thing with non-physical me?" Breia's voice trembled on the words.

"They'll have to go through every last one of us first," Maya said.

Johnny sent her a look that was a little bit surprised, but Kiley wasn't surprised at all. Ever since they'd learned about Breia's proclivities, Maya had switched from being irritated by her, to acting like her big sister.

"Thanks to Maya and Kiley's nocturnal snooping, we know they needed talismans to do whatever it is they're up to," Joe said, "And thanks to Johnny's blipping maneuver, we know they now have them. I don't think that's good. For us, at least."

"We also know there have to be boats somewhere on this island," Johnny said. "They couldn't all be gone. Nobody here would have a way off the island if that was the case."

Joe held up a finger, "Unless they arranged for the boats to be returned at a later date?"

"I think Johnny's right," Maya said.

Of course she thinks Johnny's right, Lady El put in.

"There are too many people here not to notice if all their boats suddenly went missing," Maya went on. "They're not *all* crazy, soul-stealing cult members."

"We hope," Kiley said.

"So one course of action we can take is to scour the island for a boat." Breia wrote it down. "Anyone else have anything?"

Maya nodded.

"Yeah, I have something," Joe said. "I mean, I might be more addicted than most, but I find it hard to believe this many people don't have any means to communicate with the mainland."

"There's wireless somewhere in this mansion," Maya said. "It popped up on my cell phone when we were in the depths of the house earlier, but it was password protected." She snapped her fingers. "Plus, dead Kevin radioed in when we were five minutes out, remember that?"

"That's right!" Johnny blurted it, then looked as if he hadn't meant to. "So there's a wireless connection *and* a radio around here somewhere," Kiley said.

"Find the radio and the wireless router," Breia said as she wrote it down.

"We should talk to the ghosts," Jack said. "See if they can shed any light on this." He looked around the room as he said it. "I think it's time for a seance."

"As least we have the equipment for that," Maya said.

"But no weapons," Johnny put in.

Jack said, "Notes for future reference, always have a means of self-defense because sometimes the bad guy is *not* the ghost."

"The bad guy is almost never the ghost," Kiley said. "In the meantime, let's make Johnny feel better and take stock of our arsenal. Let's see. I have hairspray and a lighter."

"I brought my athame," Maya said. "It's not supposed to be used for physical cutting, but that's a made-up rule. I don't think I'd be drummed out of witchdom for using it to stab a killer."

"I have my grandfather's hunting knife," Johnny said, then looked at Breia, who shook her head, then at Joe, who said, "I have a gun."

"*You* have a *gun*?" everyone said at once.

He nodded. "It's just a little twenty-two caliber pistol."

"I can't believe you have a gun!" Breia said.

"Well, I do."

"But why?" Kiley asked.

"My reasons are my business. And nobody here gets to judge me for them, okay?" He went to his suitcase, still on the floor, unzipped and opened it, and took out a flat black holster with a silver butt sticking out of it. "It's licensed. I took training. I used precautions, and it might be our biggest asset in this mess."

"A gun, two knives, and a hairspray blowtorch," Breia said.

"Wait a minute, wait a minute." Kiley pulled her compact out of her jeans' pocket. "This compact ...somehow Lady El can come to us through it. What if we can use it to channel the other ghosts in the same way?"

What makes you think I want some nasty ass ghosts dragging their energy into my space?

"As a last resort," Kiley added with an apologetic look into the mirror.

"Kiley's ghost-mirror," Breia said, and wrote it down. "That it?"

Everyone nodded.

"What are we going to do about Julie? "Do we keep what we know to ourselves or confront her about it?"

"Confront her," Breia said. "Demand a boat. Quit the case and go home."

"I'm with Breia," Jack said, and a chorus of "me, too" followed.

"At breakfast then," Kiley said. "That's four hours for us to wash up and catch a little sleep."

"I'll sleep first and shower later," Breia said. "I'm wiped out."

"Me, too," Johnny added.

Kiley said, "Breia, you and Maya should share the bed. Johnny and Joe, the sofa in the bedroom pulls out. You two can double up. Jack's gonna keep watch, and I'm going to grab a shower. In two hours, we'll switch out." Kiley gave orders and nobody argued.

They all headed into the bedroom, leaving her and Jack alone at last. They looked at each other and he smiled first. Then she wrapped her arms around his neck and kissed him on tiptoe. "I'm really glad we're okay." Then she tilted her head to one side, arching an eyebrow. "I mean, we're not *okay*. We're trapped on an island with a bunch of robe-wearing lunatics. But *we're* okay."

"I'm really glad too."

"Get us out of here alive and I'll make you even gladder."

He made a pistol finger at her, complete with thumb-cocking sound effect, and she headed for the shower.

CHAPTER 12

Maya woke, glanced at her phone and was surprised at the time. 5 a.m. but dark as pitch, and there was an eerie sound, a moan, a ghostly wail ... No, it was the wind. Its sound and tone were different here, filtered through palms. Back home it moved through evergreens.

The energy was different here, too. She didn't think it was due to geography alone. It was dark in this place, physically, spiritually, metaphysically and in every other imaginable way, dark.

Unease gathered low in her belly. She didn't like that feeling, that impending doom sensation. But she didn't know what to do about it just then. And Johnny was across the room. She turned her head on the pillow to look his way. He was lying on his back in a T shirt, in deference to his bedmate. She suspected he wasn't a t-shirt to bed type but their flirtation had been so brief, she'd never had the chance to find out.

Looking at him hurt. She wanted him so much, and the age thing wasn't as important to him as it was to her, but maybe she'd ruined it anyway. It certainly couldn't be solved now. Now the goal was getting off this island in one piece.

She slipped out of the bed with minimal movement, so she wouldn't wake Breia, who was curled up small beside her. She'd trembled in her sleep several times. The poor thing was terrified.

They had to get off this damn island. Today.

"So mote it be," she whispered. Then she found where she'd dropped her duffel, and took it with her into the bathroom.

There was an urgency about her shower. She cranked the knobs as if angry with them, stripped off her nightshirt, and got in before she'd even adjusted the temperature. The cold blast was welcome, and it helped clear her head. She had to set aside her emotions—Especially where Johnny was concerned, because that was a tangled-up mess in her head. It would take time and attention, unknotting all that. It deserved her full focus.

Now, though, she had to protect her friends. She had a very strong sense that Breia was in danger—that they all were. They had to get her off this island.

She cranked the taps hotter, and the heat felt good on her back and shoulders. She closed her eyes, stilled her mind for just a few seconds, focused herself fully in the moment. The flow of hot water eased her muscles, and she consciously relaxed them even more. She inhaled the warm steam and felt it cleansing her, and she pressed her feet flat to the floor and felt the power of earth's gravity holding her there. Its energy filled her, and that of the water, and the steamy air, and that of the heat suffusing her to her bones.

There. *There.*

She finished up quickly, then tiptoed through the bedroom and into the main part of the suite to relieve Kiley and Jack. Kiley was checking her phone, which was plugged into a nearby outlet, even though she had to know it was a useless effort. Jack was looking out the window.

"Why don't you guys get a couple hours sleep?" Maya said, keeping her voice low so she wouldn't wake the others. "Breakfast isn't until eight, if yesterday was the norm."

"You're on." Kiley stretched her arms over her head and arched her back. "I'm crawling in with Breia. You're on your own, babe."

"Gee, thanks," Jack said as she walked into the bedroom and closed the door softly behind her. Then he glanced Maya's way. "I don't like the looks of this weather."

"I don't like the energy of it. And Jack, Breia's shaken up. I have the feeling she has reason to be. She's in danger here. We all are, but maybe her most of all."

He nodded. "We're getting off this island, today."

"I hope so," she said. "Get some sleep. Sometimes you have to hit the reset button to get clarity."

"I'll never sleep, but I'll try." He went into the bedroom, pulling the door closed behind him.

Maya went to the window where Jack had been, and pulled back the drapes. The sun should have been up by now, but the only sign of it was more definition among the dark clouds in the distance.

Since there was no sunlight to help wake her up, she decided to resort to coffee, and went to the corner of the suite that housed its two-burner cook surface, mini-fridge, microwave, and thank the gods, coffee maker. She'd brought her own Fairtrade brew in a couple of extra-large press-and-seal teabags, which she had made herself. She got the coffee brewing, and held her mug under it instead of the carafe to catch the first cup.

The smell alone was sharpening her mind, and she bent to inhale it.

Johnny came out of the bedroom. She didn't even need to turn around before she knew it was him. But her cup was full, so she switched it for the carafe like Indiana Jones switching a bag of sand for a golden statue, and turned around to look at him.

His hair was wet and slicked back. He'd put on jeans and a gray T-shirt. He'd obviously grabbed a shower, must've been in when Jack had headed to bed. She could smell that sandalwood soap he liked.

"Good morning, Johnny."

"It's morning. I don't know how good." He lowered his head. "Sorry. Is that coffee for anyone?"

"No. It's for you." She handed him her mug, turned, took another from the shelf above the coffeemaker, and repeated her carafe swapping trick.

He took a sip while she watched it fill, and he didn't say anything until she'd replaced the carafe and turned with her mug.

"I wanted to say—"

"I owe you an apology."

They'd both spoken at once, but it was Johnny who kept going. "I've been an asshole. If you don't want to be with me, you don't want to be with me. I accept that, and I hope we can still be—"

"I want to be with you so bad I can't think straight." She blurted it in the middle of his sentence. "And I'm all mixed up about it. I'm terrified of this. I have so many doubts and questions and fears and uncertainties and—"

"Okay. Okay, Hey. He set his mug down, then took hers and set it aside, and then he hugged her. She relaxed against his chest, in the circle of his arms, and it felt so good and he smelled so good she thought if he held her long enough, she might even forget the danger they were facing. After a few seconds, he asked, "Is this okay?"

"It's *so* okay." She laid her head on his chest. "But—"

"Just a hug," he said. "I've got you. Relax. No pressure. No questions or doubts or fears need to be addressed right this minute. It's just a hug."

She relaxed even more, felt his arms tighten around her, and just soaked up his soothing, grounding energy. He was *so* connected. That was probably one of the myriad reasons he appealed to her. His spiritual nature, his curiosity about it all. He had that same reverence for life and its mystery that his grandfather had—even though they'd been estranged for his entire life.

Eventually, he let her go and she straightened up and retrieved her mug. "Man, I'm glad you told me that," he said, taking a seat in a large armchair, his mug back in his hand. "The fragile male ego I didn't know I had took a while to heal, that's all." He looked across the room at her and he smiled that smile that melted her every time. "Everything's okay."

"I'm sorry I lied to you about me and Joe. I thought you and Breia—"

"I know. But after ..." He cut himself off. "You know what, we can't have that discussion here and now. We need to focus on getting Breia and everyone else back to the mainland," he said.

"You feel it, too." It wasn't a question.

"I feel her fear. That's enough. You?"

"I feel there's a good reason for it."

"I was afraid of that."

A TAP CAME on the suite's door at seven, and it startled them both so much they jumped.

From the other side, Julie called, "Breakfast is served. We're indoors this morning. Come down whenever you're ready." Her soft steps moved away down the hall. She tapped on each door, repeating her message, not knowing the entire odd-squad had bunked in the suite in fear for their lives.

Kiley poked her head out of the bedroom a moment later. "Did somebody say breakfast?" She closed the door and opened it again in an impossibly short time, fully dressed.

Maya gave her head a shake. "You a quick-change artist now?"

"I am when there's food involved." She came out, pulled the door closed behind her. "Um, Breia doesn't want to go down there."

"I don't blame her," Johnny said. "But we can't leave her unprotected."

"Joe said he'd stay with her," Kiley went on. "And you know, he has the pistol, so ..."

Johnny looked at Maya. "I feel like I should stay, too."

She nodded. "We'll bring back food and whatever information we can get. And we won't take long about it, either," she said.

"No, we won't," Kiley agreed. "First, we're questioning Julie. Then we're scouring this island for a boat."

Jack came out of the room behind her, tucking his light blue button-down shirt into his jeans. "There's definitely a storm brewing outside," he said with a look toward the windows. Outside, the sky was dark, and the wind seemed to be whipping itself into a frenzy. "Let's get a move on before we can't."

JULIE WAS WAITING at the bottom of the staircase in a long, loose fitting white blouse with white leggings. "Apologies for the weather. It can be so unpredictable."

"I'm sure somebody radioed in a warning," Kiley said. Because why put off the confrontation? Their little death fairy had been attacked and traumatized and Kiley was good and pissed. "You know, on your radio. That you have."

"And there's internet somewhere, too," Maya said. "We got close enough that it popped up as an option last night, but it was password protected."

"What on earth are you talking about?" Julie asked, her big blue eyes all innocence. "Breakfast is this way." She turned, almost stumbled, and grabbed onto the door frame to stay upright, then steadied herself and kept going.

Looks like Johnny and Maya made up or something, Lady El said. Her mirror was sticking up out of Kiley's jeans pocket in front.

Kiley was betting on *or something.* There was no way they'd worked through their issues in the two hours they'd been on watch this morning. They both tended to think too much, in her opinion. They needed to just decide and get on with it, already.

Her stomach rumbled. "We'll discuss over breakfast," she said. "This way, is it?" She followed her nose and Julie to the right.

A short hall ended at an archway entry into a large, light room. It had ivory stucco walls, a white dining table, and a sand colored ceiling fan with palm frond shaped blades that spun lazily from a high ceiling. Even the floor tiles were light colored marble with throw rugs in darker shades of beige.

The long oval table was loaded with food and surrounded in white ladder-back chairs with green cushions. The curtains were also green.

Kiley went straight to a plate, picked it up, and moved around the table, filling it. She set it down, and repeated with a second one. "Would you have someone take this ... No, never mind, I don't trust any of your people. I'll do it myself."

"I'll do it," Maya said. She took the two plates from Kiley's hands and walked away.

Needs another minute with Johnny-cake, I bet.

"You are so mouthy."

Julie was the only one who looked at Kiley oddly. Maya walked away to deliver the food. Jack and Kiley took their seats, and Jack sent her a look that asked her to let him break the news, so she focused on gathering her own sustenance. Fruits and a pastries, coffee and juice.

"We're short on staff today," Julie said, sounding apologetic "Everyone's boarding up windows for the storm."

"A storm everyone knew about except us," Kiley said. "Funny why you'd want to keep something like that to yourself. Along with the wifi password, the existence of the radio, and where the fuck all the boats went. Isn't it?"

Jack sent her a look that told her she wasn't doing it the way he wanted, and then he addressed his ex's confused expression with news that would be certain to change the subject. "Julie, I have some terrible news," Jack said. "Kevin, the boat pilot, is dead."

"I know!" She pressed a hand to her chest. "It's so tragic, isn't it?"

"You know?" Jack asked.

"You know?" Kiley repeated.

"Of course I know, I care about the people who work for me." She pointed toward the back of the house. "Please stay away from those cliffs. They are dangerous, especially at night. Even more so in the rain."

"It wasn't raining," Kiley said. "I saw it happen. I'd been out walking with Maya. We came upon a group of people in the woods, chanting some mumbo-jumbo, all dressed in monk's robes with hoods that hid their faces. You know anything about that, Julie?"

She dropped her fork and stared across the table at her. "What in the name of God are you talking about?"

MAYA REACHED the top of the stairs with a tray full of goodness for her room-bound pals just in time to hear Breia's room door close, so she set the tray on a stand in the hall, and went over to it, opened the door and stepped in with a bright smile to see a man bent over, looking into an open dresser drawers.

"Hey!"

He whirled, stunned, and came at her. She shrieked, whipped out her phone as he charged, and rapid-tapped the camera. Then he hit her, hard, and she crashed back into the hallway, and flat onto her back on the floor. At the end of the hall, the door to the corner suite flew open, and Johnny shouted, "Hey, what the hell?"

He came running, pausing to bend over her. Joe came behind him, and rushed past, to chase the guy down.

Johnny clasped her hand. "You okay?"

"I'm good." She let him pull her up. "I was bringing you some breakfast and thought Breia was in her room, but—" She looked behind her at the stand where she'd left the tray. The coffee pot had toppled on impact, spilling onto all the food, and breaking one of the plates. Damn.

Joe came back. "I lost him. This place is like a maze. Are you all right, Maya?"

"I am." She straightened her clothes, and glanced back at Breia, who was still standing in the doorway. "Might as well come downstairs, Bray, get something to eat. It's clearly no safer up here than down there."

She nodded, then joined them in the hall. "That guy was in my room?"

"Yeah, rifling through the drawers."

She shivered and rubbed her arms, and as they headed downstairs, Maya checked her phone, but all she had captured were weird disfigured images of a face that seemed to be melting, all streaked and stretched out of shape because she'd been moving at the time.

"Useless."

Maya came back to the table but nobody was eating. Kiley and Julie were on their feet, glaring at each other across the table.

"What in the name of God are you talking about?" Julie asked.

"Six people," Kiley shot back, "one of them the late Kevin, in black-hooded robes doing some kind of mumbo-jumbo in the woods outside, is what I'm talking about."

"It's true," Maya said. "Kevin attacked me. We struggled on those cliffs and he fell."

"*You* killed Kevin?"

"Kevin killed Kevin," Johnny said.

Maya nodded hard. "Look, whoever they are, those robed people have created an energy barrier around this house that prevents non-physical beings from passing through. That's why your husband can't move through the veil to the other side. And now, why Kevin can't, either. They're both being held prisoner here. And that's a crime against the soul. That cannot be allowed to stand."

Julie looked like she thought Maya was insane.

"Where are your other two guests, Julie?" Kiley asked.

She blinked at the sudden change of subject. "They decided to go home last night. Wanted to beat the storm."

"And you didn't think we might want get the fuck off this island and *beat the storm* as well?" Kiley demanded.

"Well ...I—"

"Where are all the boats, Julie? Where's the radio, and where the fuck is the internet signal?" Kiley was clearly done playing nice.

Julie swallowed hard, and lowered her head. "Arthur didn't want any connections out here. He wanted this place to be ...unplugged."

"But you couldn't live like that," Jack said. "Could you?"

"I didn't think it was safe to be so unconnected. Especially when we ...when he got so sick. I guess I just got used to keeping it secret. I—"

"*Where*?" Kiley demanded.

"Fine. Fine, it's this way." She pushed away from the table, her breakfast uneaten. Maya grabbed a danish, filled her coffee mug, and got up to follow. Jack and Kiley came along beside her. The other three were a few beats behind, because they were starved, and grabbing food to bring along.

Julie led the way in high heeled "slippers" nobody in real life ever wears outside a Victoria's Secret shoot.

"I really didn't have any dark motivations here," Julie said. "I just ...the radio room has always been my own little secret."

"Nobody else knows about it?" Jack asked.

"Of course not."

"Then who did boat pilot Kevin think he was calling on the radio as he brought us out here?"

She brought her head up. "Well, obviously, Kevin knew. He was my most ...our most trusted employee."

"*Your* most trusted employee," Kiley said. "You had it right the first time. He was keeping your secret from your husband, so he clearly wasn't *his* most trusted anything."

Maya leaned sideways, tapping Kiley with her shoulder, and when Kiley looked at her, she made tear tracks down her cheeks with her fingers, then pointed ahead at Julie, who had clearly been crying. She figured Kiley was too pissed off to pay much attention. They'd traversed one long hallway and turned down another, this one curving to the right.

"It must have been hard on you, losing Kevin," Maya said.

Her tone was friendlier than Kiley's. One caught more flies with sugar than with vinegar, right?

Julie nodded without looking behind her. "He's been with us a long time."

"How long?"

She didn't reply, instead stopping at a door with a keypad on the outside. Kiley watched her fingers tap keys and memorized the four digits before the door swung open.

"What does Arthur think this room is?" Jack asked. "You must've told him something."

She shrugged one shoulder, stepped in and turned on a light switch and then gasped and covered her mouth with one hand at the demolished equipment. A short-wave radio with its console crushed, assorted bits and pieces everywhere, and a sledge hammer, the likely culprit, lying on the floor over a laptop with its screen torn off its base.

"What the hell *is* this?" Julie asked, and she turned accusing eyes on them. "Are *you* responsible for this?"

"We're the ones who *want* the radio, dumbass."

Jack was already past Kiley examining pieces and parts while four of them stayed out of the small room, looking in from the hall.

"Can it be fixed?" Kiley asked.

"Maybe if we'd brought Chris, but ..." Jack examined the equipment and picked up a thoroughly flattened piece. "This was the modem." Then he tossed it back onto the floor.

"Oh my God," Julie whispered. "Oh my God, we're really cut off."

"*We've* been cut off the whole time, as far as we knew," Kiley pointed out. "Not a nice way to treat the team who came here to help you."

"I've apologized for keeping it from you. Will you let it go, already?"

"I will *not* let it go. If you knew me at all, you would know that I *never* let *anything* go."

Everyone muttered validation of that fact. From the look Kiley sent to her ever-present and ever-opened gold compact, even Lady El had agreed.

Then Maya said, "Okay so there's no radio and no internet—for real this time. Let's accept it and move on to step two. Getting the hell off this island."

Julie sent a wounded look Jack's way, but he only nodded. "She's right. We have to go. Now why don't you tell us where you've hidden the boats?"

"Hidden?" She gaped at him, then at Kiley and Maya. "What are you accusing me of, exactly?"

"You want a list?" Kiley asked.

"What the hell is your problem, Kiley? Is it jealousy? Is that it?"

"*Jealousy*?" Kiley's eyes were not green. Red, maybe, like right before a vampire attacks. "You think *I'm* jealous of *you*?"

"He married me. I don't see a ring on your finger."

"I will rip your tonsils out through your nose, you cocky little—"

"Whoa-kay now." Maya stepped in front of Julie, blocking her while Jack put his hands on Kiley's shoulders to keep her from giving his ex a makeover—with her fists. "Just tell us where the boats are and we can go our separate ways." Maya made her voice all reasonable again. She hated having to be the reasonable one, but when you worked with Kiley, it was kind of a given.

"It's a tropical storm, you idiots!" Julie cried. "Nobody in their right mind would take a boat out in this. Not even Arthur would've ..." The words tripped over a sob, and she couldn't finish. She left the room, pushing her way through all of them, flipping the lights off behind her, leaving them to follow.

"Look," Jack said, leading the pursuit. "We need to figure out who the six people in the monk's robes were."

"Five," Kiley said. "One was Kevin."

"After Kevin attacked me on the cliffs, the others chased Breia and scared her half to death," Maya said.

"That's not possible, Kevin wouldn't—"

"Not only would he, but he did," Jack said, and it sounded like even his boundless patience was finally running low. "My people don't lie. There's some kind of cult group conjuring dark energies on this island, Julie, and it's hard to believe you could live here and not know about it. Furthermore, we're aware the missing jewelry you asked us to find is a pile of gold talismans that this cult group has already found."

"That's not true. There aren't any cultists. Nothing like that is going on and if there was, Arthur would have ..." She stopped there, back in the dining room, hands on the back of her chair, blinking as her brows pressed close.

"Arthur would have what?" Jack prompted.

Nobody sat down. Kiley helped herself to another danish, though.

"Arthur would've known."

"But not you?" he asked. He'd gentled his tone again. Maya could tell by her scowl that Kiley didn't like it one bit.

Julie shook her head. "I haven't been ...I haven't been living here. I didn't come out until ...just before the end."

"You were estranged," Maya said, and Julie nodded.

Julie pulled out her chair and sat down, as if determined to eat her breakfast. She had a poached egg perched in a fancy holder. It was probably cold.

"C'mon, Julie. Tell us," Kiley said, because it probably was, now that Maya had pointed it out.

"You're out of your minds." Julie sighed heavily. "We had a brief disagreement, but we were reunited and deliriously happy before he ..." She let her voice trail off. "You might as well eat. You can't leave."

She tapped her egg's shell with a spoon until it cracked and began to peel it.

Everyone sat down and dug in. The food was cold, but it was mostly meant to be. There were lots of pre-cut fruits, a platter of pastries.

Kiley refiled her mug and passed the pot to her left, even though that meant handing it to Julie.

She said, "There were some books on the occult in Arthur's studio that I'd never seen before. I found them while straightening up one day. He was sleeping, but he woke and saw me with them and he got irrationally upset." Shrugging one shoulder, she said, "The hospice nurse said it was normal, that the stress of dying—"

"I think we'd better take another look around Arthur's studio," Maya said.

Jack nodded. "And I think I'd better make an all-out effort to have a heart-to-heart talk with Arthur."

"Just so it's clear," Maya said, "We are leaving this island the instant it's safe to do so. So we'll need to know where the boats are."

"The boats are in the boathouse. Where else would they be with a hurricane coming?"

"I thought you said tropical storm," Maya said. Suddenly she wasn't so hungry anymore.

CHAPTER 13

"Wait." Julie rushed after them when they all headed for the staircase. "I'm coming with you." She gave a look behind her and rubbed her arms.

The curtains were all closed tight, and you couldn't see outside, but the wind had begun to pick up, and it moaned ever louder.

Tell her to go piss up a rope, Lady El said.

Kiley bent her chin to her chest. "Is that even a thing?"

"Come with us, then," Breia said. "It's dark as a dungeon in here and the wind's starting to howl. I'd be scared to be alone, too."

"Don't you have to board up windows or something?" Kiley asked. Maya elbowed her in the ribs but Lady El laughed.

"It's all automated. Once the winds hit forty-five, the shutters self-deploy."

Of course they do.

Lady El was an excellent girlfriend, Kiley decided. Then she shrugged and continued up the stairs. Jack hadn't even slowed down, but she caught up before he veered off into the wing that wasn't their own. Maya came along three steps behind them, and the others followed.

"Do you think she's telling the truth?" Jack asked as they went through the double doors into Arthur's bedroom—the one he had abandoned for the studio above it. That was where he'd wanted to spend his final days, up in the studio with the 360° view of his own personal paradise. It was almost poetic.

"I think she's lying through her teeth," Kiley said. "But I'm aware my opinion is completely colored by my seething dislike of her."

"Are you really jealous?" he asked. Straight to the point, didn't even beat around the bush first. He'd been hanging out with her too long, she thought.

She decided to answer the same way. "Probably."

Wouldn't anyone be? She's a knockout zillionaire widow. Who can compete with that?

Kiley glared down at the mirror in her pocket, and Lady El lifted her eyebrows in mock innocence.

Besides you, I meant.

"Sure you did."

They moved through the suite and started up the spiral staircase to the upper level. Kiley tried, illogically, to be quiet like you do at a funeral, but that was an impossible feat on the noisy metal stairs. Every step clanged like a cowbell. They emerged into the upper level, and Kiley immediately felt dizzy, and reached for the nearest solid object, which turned out to be Jack's chest. He had a freaking awesome chest. Leaves and twigs and other debris swirled outside the windows, making it feel as if the room itself was spinning.

"Here, over here." Jack covered her hand with his and brought her away from the stairs, probably afraid she'd keel over and bounce all the way back down. He nodded at a chair, but Kiley decided to sit on the floor, to avoid the seasick sensation.

Maya came up, Johnny right behind her, and she said, "Holy god," and reached out a hand for balance, just like Kiley had. Johnny wobbled a little, then put his arm around Maya's shoulders to steady them both. They came and sat beside Kiley while Jack went around closing all the blinds. And because the circle of Scoobs on the floor was already under construction, so to speak, Joe and Breia sat there, too.

Julie didn't. She came up last of all, and slowly, holding on to the railing as if to pull herself along. When she came through into the upper level, Kiley noticed that her stupid high heel slippers with the feathers on the toes were now dangling from her hands.. She dropped them onto the floor, went directly to the cube of wood that passed for a desk and braced her arms on it, hanging her head between them. Once she got her balance again, she straightened up and moved to one of the windows to open the blinds Jack had just closed. Apparently, the view of the storm was one she wanted to see.

"It's bad," she said. "Last forecast I heard said it might hit category one by landfall."

"You really should've told us," Jack said.

"I know. I'm ...sorry. Look, to be honest, I was scared to be here alone. I know Arthur is here, and he's ...angry, I think."

A bird crashed into the glass and she jumped backward, biting her shriek off halfway, then pressed her fingers to her forehead and closed her eyes.

No doubt about it, she was nervous as hell. The question was why? Kiley doubted she was scared of her dead husband. Every other time Arthur had been brought up, she'd seemed sad, and still-devoted.

Jack went past her and lowered the blinds once more.

Maya said, "Thanks, Jack. This place makes me seasick." Then she got up and went to the free standing wooden bookshelves and dragged her fingers over rows of spines. "Where is this book that he got so upset about?"

"Not on the shelf," Julie said. "It's hidden, that's what caught my attention." She crossed the room to a tilted drafting table. It was hinged so it could be angled perfectly for the artist. She flipped a catch, and turned it vertically, revealing a square box attached underneath. Opening its lid, Julie removed a book from within and held it out at arm's length.

Maya took it. Kiley was too busy noticing that there were other books in there with it before Julie closed the lid and flipped the tabletop back down.

Maya returned to her spot on the floor and started flipping through the book.

"So, you really left out a lot when you hired us," Jack said.

"She left out everything," Kiley added

He nodded at her in agreement. "Would you like to start over? Tell us everything this time?"

"So we stand a snowball's chance in hell of helping you?" Kiley added.

He reels her in and you throw her back, sweetie. Maybe you should let Jack do the talking.

"I am seriously rethinking how good a girlfriend you are, El."

"I'm sorry, what?" Julie asked.

"Nothing." Kiley crossed her arms and handed off to Jack with a look that said, "Back to you."

He smiled and sent a well-aimed wink toward her jeans pocket and Lady El giggled like a bashful schoolgirl.

Maya's eyes were speeding over the pages of the book that lay open on her lap. The rest of them focused on Julie, and even Kiley kept her trap shut and paid attention to her story.

∾

"WE WERE ESTRANGED," Julie began. "He told me that he had come to believe I'd only married him for his money, said he was leaving, and I could have the house. Said he was coming out to the island and asked for his space. I knew it was a lie."

"How?" Jack asked.

"I snooped. Found his medical bills and test results. He was dying and he knew it. I thought he wanted to spare me going through his final days." She shook her head slowly. "But that wasn't true, either. I came out here, and he was angry. Said all he wanted was some privacy, some time to himself, but I refused to leave, and it was a good thing, because he got too sick to get by on his own. I hired him a nurse, managed the place, took care of the staff, did everything I could to make his last days easier, all while running his business remotely. Which is why I needed the wireless. He had his bed moved up here, refused to come into the rest of the house at all. Got mad every time I came up, cursed me, threw things. So I mostly stayed in the main house and left him alone." A tear leaked from the corner of her eye, and she quickly pressed her finger to soak it up as if she didn't want anyone to see it. "I knew it wasn't really him, but the dying process. He no longer even cared about his life's work, his passions, his painting, nothing." She lowered her head. "Not even me."

Kiley thought she might be telling the truth. You didn't generally manufacture a tear only to wipe it away before anyone could see it.

True, Lady El said. *You let it roll slowly down your cheek and make sure* everyone *sees it.*

"After a while, though, he was too sick to object, and on too much morphine to know or care who was in here. So I started coming in to straighten up while he was sleeping, check his IV and his catheter, turn him in the bed, all the things the private nurse used to do before he fired her in a fit of temper. He slept through my visits most of the time. But that one day, that one day when I found the book, he came full awake and roared at me. I didn't think there was enough strength left in him to yell like that."

Kiley definitely thought she was telling the truth. She shivered and paled with the memory.

"He died three days later. Left me everything in the will, including this place. I was going to sell it right after the funeral and never set foot here again, but ...things started happening."

"What kinds of things?" Kiley asked.

She rubbed her arms and finally sat on the floor with the rest of them, curling her legs to one side beneath her. "Footsteps up here, back and forth, like he was pacing. Sometimes there would be a loud thud or a crash. Sometimes I swore the bed was wrinkled, as if someone had been sitting on it. Sometimes pieces of art would be thrown on the floor or even torn. I swore I could feel his anger and frustration."

"He's trapped," Breia said. "He can't move on. I think that occult group trapped his spirit here for some reason, same as they trapped Kevin's. What I can't figure out is why."

"Maybe he trapped his own spirit here," Maya said. "This book is about soul transferal. It talks about about keeping a soul from crossing over when the body dies, in order to transfer it into another body. Maybe one that's young and healthy and strong."

"Oh come on. You don't think anyone would believe something like that could actually work." Joe sounded skeptical.

"Well, the soul-entrapment part clearly works," Maya said. "That's obviously what the barrier is for."

"Ahhhhh," Kiley said, drawing out the sound. Everyone nodded.

"The part about getting into another body—"

"He didn't get the chance to find out," Julie said, moving

back to that cube desk, which seemed to be her favorite spot, the way she gravitated to it. Maybe it was solid and grounding for her. Damn, Kiley thought, she'd been hanging around with Maya too long. "Where would he get a body?"

"But ...it couldn't work even with a body," Joe said. "If it were feasible, then a person could attain immortality that way. Just keep changing bodies when one wears out. Theoretically, at least. If that were possible, people would've been trying it by now."

"Maybe that's exactly what we've stumbled upon here," Maya said. "People trying to make it work." She frowned hard. "Is anyone here on the island, any of your staff or even your other guests, sick or facing mortality in any way?" she asked Julie. "Tilda Carlisle, she must be what ...sixty-five? That's not that old, yet she seems frail."

"Recurring heart failure," Julie said. "And Horace is on the transplant list for a new kidney. He only has one, and it's failing."

"But he seemed so healthy," Breia whispered.

"Twice a week dialysis keeps him functional."

"Do you think he was involved? Maybe both of them?"

Julie shrugged. "He spent a lot of time up here with Arthur. They both did. Talking and talking, all the time talking. I always wondered what about."

Maya nodded, still skimming pages. "Cheating death does seem to be the goal," she said softly. "Maybe that's why he didn't want you up here, Julie. Maybe he was trying to keep it from you."

"It can't work, though," Breia said. "It's unnatural."

"The talismans are a part of it," Maya said, reading on. And she sounded as fascinated as she did terrified. She read aloud from the book. "The talisman is engraved with its owner's personal sigil, and those representing immortality, soul trans-feral, and divine power over other mortals. It must then be dressed with three drops of its owner's blood in a full ritual on the night of a dark moon, void of course.'" She lifted her head. "That would be a very short window." Then she read on. "The talisman, placed upon the replacement of a living body, lends it supernatural strength and endurance. And when is placed on a newly dead body, one from which the soul has emerged, the talisman guides its owner's soul in to replace the one that has gone."

"How do they get the original soul out?" Breia asked, her eyes round and frightened.

"The usual way, I would imagine," Julie said.

"My grandfather said death cannot be cheated." Johnny sounded a lot like his grandfather when he quoted the man, which was often. His voice was deeper, slower, more deliberate. "It could be delayed perhaps, but never avoided. He said that mankind's quest for immortality would be what would eventually lead to our destruction."

"Given what happened with my parents, I have to agree with your grandfather," Breia said softly.

No one had heard from John Redhawk for months. But the last word he'd sent to Johnny—a postcard with a Budapest postmark—had said not to worry, and that he would return when he'd done what he had to do. He'd asked for time and privacy and promised he would see them all again soon.

Kiley was worried anyway. They all were. Come on, Budapest?

The wind howled louder. Kiley wondered if the third story was the safest place to be. But suddenly there was a mechanical hum, and dark panels slid slowly from left to right across the outside of the windows. Another level of darkness laid itself over the room, probably over the entire house as the automatic shutters moved into place with an ominous and final-sounding clang.

Johnny said, "They were putting a necklace on Kevin's body in that cave. A talisman, maybe."

The shutters deadened the noise of the storm, but then another sound came. The unmistakable sound of footsteps coming up that noisy metal staircase.

CHAPTER 14

Everyone got to their feet and squeezed in close. Kiley had a death grip on Jack. Maya stood beside Johnny. Breia had moved behind Joe, who was much taller, so she was completely hidden back there.

Kevin the boat pilot's head appeared first as he climbed the staircase, and Kiley gulped because it seemed to be attached by a painfully crooked neck. His skin was blue-gray, and his eyes looked out from behind a blue film.

What in hell is that? Lady El asked, whispering even though nobody but Kiley could hear her.

Kevin smiled as he came the rest of the way up, and it was so creepy, Breia screamed.

"What's going on?" Julie asked. "Kevin?" She took a step closer. Kiley thought she was either brave or stupid. Personally, she was thinking about heading out onto the balcony and taking her chances with the hurricane.

"Guess again, sugar."

Julie's feet froze where they were. She blinked at him. "What ...why did you call me that? Only Arthur called me that."

"It's me, love, don't you recognize me? It's your old, dead husband."

"Ah-ah ...Arthur?"

He was standing near the stairs. He nodded on that crooked neck, and his head wasn't centered like it should be, so the motion was grotesque. His arms and legs were bent at weird angles, too.

"B-but ...omygod, Arthur, is it really you? But ...Kevin's body—"

"Was already dead, I know. Any port in a storm, isn't that the saying?" He looked down at the book opened on the floor. "It works, Julie." He took a step toward her, and she took one backward. "It really works. I've come back to you."

"I can't. Not in that body, not like this. God, Arthur, it smells."

He laughed and it was the creepiest thing Kiley had ever seen. "Why did you bring these people here?"

He reached for her, but she stepped backward, tears streaming.

Kiley sidestepped right in front of her, pulling Jack with her. "You're not getting near her, asshole."

"Oh, you're protecting her. That's so cute." But his eyes went back to Julie. "You thought they could learn where I'd hidden the other talismans." He said it like an accusation.

Julie nodded, a staccato motion of her head that seemed convulsive. She was still backing up, though.

"You should've trusted me, Julie. I trusted you. It was the others I doubted. But I never lost faith in you." She was standing with her back to the solid wooden desk. The others closed ranks in front of her, and Maya said, "You'll have to go through all of us, and that's not gonna be easy, considering your condition."

"It's true, this body is a mess."

"It was already dead," Breia whispered from behind Joe.

"Dead is dead. This whole soul transferal thing you're trying to pull off, it won't work—not like that."

"I had to give it a try. It was getting harder to stay focused. When the pretty blonde here threw Kevin to his death—"

"He attacked us," Maya said. "All we did was defend ourselves."

The corpse shrugged. Bones cracked and popped. "It seemed the perfect opportunity. "My friends of questionable loyalty performed the ritual to pull my soul into Kevin's body once his was out. I'd have used my own, but it was taken away for burial before I realized there would be a time limit on occupying a re-animated corpse."

"Then why the hell keep Kevin's soul prisoner?" Kiley asked.

"Because it's his turn next. And unlike some others, I'm a man of my word. I promised him a new body. I promised each of the others the same. They're all facing their own mortality in one way or another. Kevin had early onset Alzheimers," he said. "He really didn't want to go out like that."

"Kevin has changed his mind," Johnny said. "Death has a way of clarifying things, for most people."

He looked beside him as he said it, and when Jack's hand on Kiley's arm tightened, she knew he could see Kevin's ghost.

He just floated up those stairs, Lady El cried. *He's angry!*

"He wants you to let him go," Jack said. "And he wants his body laid to rest. Maybe you should vacate it."

"As the winged-one said, I'm not going to be able to last long in here anyway. Julie is right, it's starting to smell." Arthur laughed, but the mouth didn't smile, just opened to emit the sound, and the stench that emerged with it made Kiley gag. "What I need, you see, is a body that *isn't* dead. One I can move into while its soul is ...out and about."

"Oh God he means me. He means me," Breia cried. And Kiley turned to look at her, but it was Julie who caught her eye.

She was leaning on the cube of a desk so heavily it was as if she wished she could crawl inside.

"Actually, I mean all of you."

Kiley's head came back around to focus on the dead guy who'd just threatened their lives.

"Sorry, pal," Jack said. "Our bodies are all in use right now. Our no-vacancy sign is on."

A sound, a movement had Kiley looking behind her again. Then she swore fluently, because the cube desk was three feet further to the left than it had been before. Julie had pushed it sideways, and the floor beneath it was open. Hooded figures were coming up from the stairway that stupid cube desk had apparently hidden.

"Nicely done, Julie," Arthur said, from Kevin's body.

Joe spun around, spotted the hooded cultists, and pushed Breia behind him. Then he hauled off and punched the first one that emerged, right in the face. It fell backward with a yelp, but another came up right behind and caught her as her hood fell backward, revealing Tilda Carlisle, and there was no doubt to the identity of the man who'd caught her. His shape gave him away. Horace Stoltz.

Jack shoved Arthur in Kevin's body, and he toppled to the floor like a Jenga tower, then he grabbed Kiley's hand and pushed her toward the spiral staircase. "Go, Kiley! Get out of here, now!"

Arthur-Kevin grabbed Jack's ankles and yanked them right out from under him. He hit the floor face-first. Horace and Joe were wrestling for Joe's gun, which he'd pulled, but never managed to fire.

Breia shot past them all and shot down the spiral stairs. Kiley looked back at Maya, but one of the hoodies had hold of her. Another had grabbed Johnny, and a third threw something on the floor that exploded in a blast of white smoke.

Johnny wrested free of the one who held him. Kiley realized as one of the hoods fell down that it was Beasley, the cook, and wondered how the hell she had been so strong. Part of whatever black magic they'd been working, she assumed. As she looked on, the cultists replaced their hoods with gas masks. They handed extra masks to Arthur and Julie.

Johnny got free of Beasley and lunged to grab Tilda, who had Maya around the neck. He yanked Tilda off and yelled, "Go!"

Then he started coughing and so did Maya. This was bad.

Kiley grabbed Maya's arm and pulled her out of the white smoke, covering her nose and mouth with her free hand. Julie was hitting a button on the wall, and a low groan came from the floor above the spiral staircase—a trapdoor, mechanized like the shutters, was sliding slowly over the opening.

Maya pushed Kiley ahead of her, and she fell onto the upper stairs before the opening sealed above her with Maya still on the other side. Kiley pounded on the door above her head. She could hear her friends coughing and choking on the other side. But it was no good. It wouldn't budge.

"There was another stairway under that desk!" Breia cried, gripping Kiley's hand from behind. "We can get in that way! We just have to find where it goes."

"Oh I think I know where it goes," Kiley said. "And those fuckers are going to be sorry when they head back down there, because we'll be waiting."

She turned and squeezed past Breia on the narrow metal staircase, grabbing her hand on the way. "Come on."

Breia pulled her hand free. "I could get back up there. I could pop out of my body and float right back up there."

"No, no way. Then one of them will show up out of some other hidden passage around this joint to take over your body while you're out of it. That's exactly what they want. No way,

Bray. We're not making it that easy on them. Come on, come with me."

"We can't just leave them."

"We can't save them if we're up there with them. Come on, I have a plan."

MAYA SAW Johnny fall to the floor. Joe was already there. She pulled her blouse up over her face, and looked for something to use as a weapon. Her eyes were burning. Jack was struggling with two of the cultists, all of whom were wearing gas masks. Her eyes were burning and her lungs were on fire. She stumbled, fell, got up onto her hands and knees, and crawled nearer to where Johnny lay on the floor. The opening under the desk was just ahead. She could drag him there, and through it, and—

And then she fell flat, her face on Johnny's chest, and wondered if the gas was lethal.

"They're all out," somebody said. She thought it was Kevin-Arthur. "Open a window."

"But the storm—" That was Julie, for sure. Kiley had been right about that bitch all along. What an actress. She'd had them all fooled. God, to think how they'd all tried to protect her, there, at the last.

"Fuck the storm and open the window," Arthur said. "And the rest of you, bring up the supplies. We need to do the ritual *now*. This body is running out of time."

Maya heard the wind howl louder when Julie opened one of the windows. It whipped in powerfully, and she turned her face toward it, hoping her movement was hidden by her arms, which framed her head on Johnny's chest.

She opened her eyes very slightly. Julie, Arthur in Kevin's body, and one of the hooded folks were taking off their gas masks. The other two must've gone back down into the opening under the desk. There was nowhere else in this room they could hide.

Johnny was out cold beneath her. Breia and Kiley had made it out. They'd be back. They would make a rescue attempt. No way were these maniacs going to steal their bodies. It wasn't possible, it wouldn't work. But they could damn well kill them in the process of trying.

"Julie, do you have the kit?"

Julie went to the mini-fridge in the corner, making Maya wish she'd looked more closely at the vials inside. She took several of them out, and set them side by side on the drafting table. "What do I do now, Arthur?" she asked. "How is this going to work?"

Kevin's body moved closer to her, like a scarecrow with its parts on wrong. Its gait was uneven and lumbering, its arms and legs broken, and its neck even more crooked than before. Outside, the wind screamed and carried litter and debris into the room with it, but the smoke had cleared rapidly, and the fresh air cooled Maya's eyes and soothed her lungs.

The walking dead man reached out with his backward arm, and tried to pick up one of the vials, but only knocked it over. He released a stream of cuss words as Julie quickly picked up the vial, looked at the label, and placed it back on the table.

"That one stops the heart," the crooked man said. "And the other re-starts it. We'll need to keep their hearts stopped long enough for their souls to leave their bodies, and ours move in to take their place. But not a second longer." Then he smiled at Julie. "I'm glad you brought these people here to try to find out where I'd hidden the talismans, sugar. It turned out to be kismet, didn't it? As if it were meant to be."

"I still don't know why you hid them," she said. "If you were going to keep your promise to them anyway."

"Because," he said, "They grew sick of waiting for me to die and killed me."

Julie gasped, her eyes going wide.

"They were deteriorating, all of them. They wanted to jump the line, you see. But you were suffering too, my love, and yet you cared for me. You never tried to hasten my death."

"Because I love you, Arthur," she said.

"And that's why the two of us will go first."

Wait, Maya thought. What the hell was wrong with Julie? Was she also dying?

The two missing figures came up from the stairway that had formerly been hidden by the cube desk, their monk's robes and cavernous hoods in place.

"Hurry it up," Arthur-Kevin shouted over the wind. "They'll be coming around soon. Julie, close the window now."

She scrambled to do what he told her, and Maya wondered what was in all of this for her. The two unidentified asshats opened the ornate wooden box they carried, and began removing black candles from it. They were big, chunky pillars that would stand on their own without need of holders. They began setting them on the floor, and Maya knew they were going to form a circle around her and her friends. While they worked, Tilda and Julie dragged Joe and Jack closer to her Johnny, and dropped them without a care. When Jack's head clunked onto the floor, Arthur-Kevin said, "That's *my* head you're hurting, Ladies." Then he looked at Julie. "That's the body you prefer me to take, yes my love?"

"I like the other one better," Julie said. "That long dark hair, and he's younger, too. He'll last longer."

Maya thought there must be smoke coming out of her ears.

"That one then," the walking corpse said.

When the circle of candles was complete, other items came out of the chest. A statue of some horned demon Maya had never seen before. Just another false god invented by man and used to scare others into obeying their religion's dictates. He was given horns to associate him with ancient nature gods like Pan and Herne, to depict them as devils. Gods of the woodlands and wild things, gods of nature and love, re-cast as fallen angels turned evil. Powerful now. Real now. Brought to life by the belief of mankind.

They placed the demon figures amid the circle of candles, facing inward. One of the statues had ruby eyes that seemed to be looking right at Maya.

Fuck you, Satan. You even suck as a myth, she thought as loudly as she could. But she was scared, because she knew that a myth given a lot of attention, a lot of thought, a lot of focus, a lot of belief, becomes real over time. A thought-form becomes something physical. It's how all creation came to be. First an idea, then attention to the idea, then the thing. Everything from the wheel to the Large Hadron Collider was first a thought. This devil they apparently worshipped could pose a real problem.

She closed her hand a little, digging her nails into Johnny's chest.

"I assume you want her, body, correct?" Arthur-Kevin asked with a nod Maya's way.

"She's beautiful and blonde like me. And no sign of MS."

MS. Of course! Maya recalled each time Julie had seemed weak-kneed or clumsy and realized she wasn't either of those things. She was sick, too.

They were both looking at Maya then, so she kept her eyes closed and her body very still, while inside she was anything but quiet. She was calling on the Dark Mother, the goddess of death, inviting Her in, channeling Her. The harvester of souls. The mistress of the underworld, the queen of the dead. She did not take kindly to mortals usurping Her authority.

"Where the hell are the oils? We need the oils!" Arthur raged.

"They're not in the box?" Beasley asked in her accented voice. "This has to work, Arthur. It has to. I'm weaker every day, I know it's getting worse."

Something smashed into the shutters that covered the windows, and she squawked—you could not call it a scream—and cowered with her arms over her head. "The storm is getting worse."

"The house will hold. It's held through a cat four, it won't buckle from a one. And your body will hold. Our dark rites and your talisman have given you the strength of the gods, if only for a few hours."

"I think I should go first." She blurted the words so fast it was almost as if she was afraid to say them. "I'm the closest to death."

"Arthur is *already* dead," Julie said, and her tone was sharp. "I'd say that's a little closer. Now go below and get the oils! And make it fast! We don't have much time."

Beasley vanished back down the hidden staircase with Tilda following on her heels.

Horace crouched near Maya, pulled her hands behind her, and tied them with a rough rope, yanking the knot so tight she had to bite her lip to keep from wincing.

"Those are my wife's wrists you're trying to break, Horace. Do you even *want* a body for yourself?"

"I want the tall body. I've always wished to be taller."

"Try taking care of it this time. His kidneys are fine now, but if you soak them in booze, they'll wear out as fast as your own did."

"Then it will be time for another, won't it?" Horace laughed. He was drunk on the power surging through him, Maya thought. Dark power. They'd tapped into something, for sure. Something evil. The darkest intentions of humanity.

Well, she could tap into power, too. In her mind, the Dark goddesses swirled around her, morphing from one into the other as they circled in her mind's eye. They circled just as the storm circled. They *were* the storm. Maya spoke with her heart, knowing they could hear. *Hecate. Freya. Ereshkigal. Morrigan. Hel. Coatlicue. Goddess of the storm that rages around me even now. Come and hear my cry. Come and lend your might. Come and thwart those who would steal the power that is yours alone.*

"Where the hell are Tilda and Beasley with the oils?" The dead man said.

KILEY AND BREIA pulled on raincoats they found hanging in the kitchen, then ran out into the ferocity of the storm. The rain slashed in sideways, and the wind was in their faces. She and Breia locked arms and bent into it. She wished she'd gone for a flashlight, but she hadn't thought there would be time. They followed the wide, winding path down to the beach, but it was so dark and windy they could only tell when they'd veered off it by the weeds and brush along one side, and the boulders off the other. It was a dangerous walk down the cliff-path, amid the rocks. Kevin had died in a fall from the very place they now traversed, and there'd been no raging storm then.

"The cave," Breia said, shouting over the storm to Kiley. "You think the stairway under the desk leads to the cave."

"That's what I think," Kiley shouted back. They trudged on, around a sharp curve in the path, cutting through the woods, where the wind made a keening wail through the trees, but even so, the strong trunks and dense foliage provided relief from the worst it. And yet it was dangerous. Limbs were crashing to the ground around them with every few steps they took. One would smash just behind, then one just ahead. It was only by sheer luck they made it through unscathed.

They rounded a large boulder and quickly located the stone face that was false. The one Johnny had somehow opened before. It was closed and they had no time.

Kiley ran her hands along one side. Her hood fell backward, and rain soaked her hair and face, but she didn't stop to pull it back up. Beside her, Breia was doing the same, searching for a switch, a lever, something. Kiley pressed a rounded cobble that moved inward at her touch. The cave door slid silently open on ball bearings in tracks in the earth. She locked her arm with Breia's and stepped into the mouth of the cave. And the instant they did, the wind and rain stopped its assault. The stone door slid closed on its own behind them, and the cave was dark midnight.

Locked arm-in-arm, they pressed on, moving deeper into the tunnel below the earth. It was a relief to be out of the wind and rain. Kiley stopped just long enough to shrug out of the wet, borrowed coat.

Breia did the same.

"Here, we'll shove them behind that boulder, out of sight. We need weapons."

"Like what?" Breia looked around the dark cave, finally picking up a softball sized rock.

Kiley picked up two of them, then nodded at Breia. It might've been ten minutes since they'd left the house, but it felt like hours. Crouching low, they crept still deeper into the cave, and that's when they heard the sound of footsteps and voices up ahead.

MAYA SANK her nails into Johnny's chest, willing him to wake up. She was watching Julie fill syringes and line them up on the drafting cube desk that had hidden the stairway. She noted that some had red labels, others green, and that Julie lined them up in pairs, one of each color.

One to stop the heart, and one to restart it.

Maya shivered as she recalled that statement.

"There's no more time," Arthur-Kevin said, and his words were slurred as if he were drunk. "This body is dying ..."

"We need the oils to do it properly, though," Julie said. "You said we'd have to draw the sigil of Lucifer on the new body's head in the thrice-blessed oil," she argued. "Just give them a few more minutes—"

"I said *now!*" And he lunged, grabbed a red syringe, and jammed it into Johnny's neck so fast, Maya couldn't prevent her reaction.

She grabbed his hand and shouted "No!"

"You bitch!" Julie said, and she lunged, too, jabbing a needle into Maya's chest.

Maya gasped, her eyes flying wide.

Horace said, "What about the rest of us?"

"Oversee our transferal, and then we'll oversee yours," Julie said. "You're not skipping the line like you planned! You faithless idiot." She took the talisman from around her own neck, and leaned over to put it around Maya's.

Maya panicked, yanking so hard on her bonds that somehow, her hands came free, and she slapped Julie across the face. Then came a powerful squeezing sensation in her chest. She sucked in three open-mouthed breaths, pressing her hand to her heart. Julie grabbed her arm and pulled her away from Johnny. Dead Kevin was leaning over him, taking the talisman from his own neck and putting in on Johnny's.

Julie arranged Maya flat on the floor within the circle, as she clung to consciousness. Then she grabbed what seemed like a handful of syringes from the table, and stretched out beside her, while Horace hurried around lighting the candles.

Arthur, in Kevin's body, came into the circle, too, but he struggled to move. He'd step with one leg, then drag the other. He was looming over Johnny when Maya's vision went dark, but it was brief, the darkness. Like blinking.

And then she was awake and alert and able to move freely. She reached for Johnny, who was still lying there on the floor, and wondered why she wasn't. She didn't remember getting up. She touched his face, but her hand moved right through.

"Maya," he whispered, but not from there. Not from where she was trying to touch him. Not from his beautiful body.

She lifted her head and saw him, but he was different. He was translucent and glowing as if lit from within. He smiled at her, and she looked down at her hands, turning them palm up in wonder at the way they glowed. She felt light, and suffused with a sense of freedom she could not previously have imagined.

Then she looked lower, and saw her body lying there on the floor, within the ring of black candles and leering demons, and widened her eyes. "Are we dead?"

"I don't feel dead," Johnny told her. He touched her face and she felt it. "I don't feel like what's going on down there much matters, though. I feel like everything's okay, either way."

"I feel that way, too. It's so odd. We should be raging and fighting and—"

"You're the most beautiful thing I've ever seen," Johnny said.

He was looking at her with adoring eyes, and there was white light beaming from him to her and from her to him. The two beams met and melded, and she felt it. She felt his love as a real thing, warm and thick, sweet and soothing.

He moved closer, and she reached for him, and then they twisted around each other from head to toe, except their heads and their toes were only illusions. He whispered, "I love you. I love you beyond anything that exists."

And she said, "I love *you*. I love you purely and fully and endlessly." It felt so good to be entwined with him this way. It felt like a reunion with a part of herself she'd been missing and yearning for, never knowing what or why.

As they held each other, there was a sound, steady and growing louder. It was a drumbeat, she realized, and without separating herself from Johnny, she sought its source.

And then she saw him. John Redhawk. Johnny's grandfather. He was sitting by a fire in a beautiful forest, pounding a steady beat on a hand drum. Johnny saw him too, and she felt everything he felt, the joy of having found his grandfather at last, of reuniting with him, and the wonder of how this could be.

Maya wondered, too. She and Johnny were in a mansion, on an island, in a hurricane. Or had been. Now they seemed to be floating far above all that, somehow. Above the storm, even. John was in a quiet and peaceful forest, where barely a breeze disturbed the trees. His eyes were closed. He seemed unaware of their presence until, still drumming that steady cadence, he spoke.

"The spirit is vast. It can see all places, all times. Hear my voice, grandson. Listen to the beat of the drum. Follow where it leads."

CHAPTER 15

M aya didn't want to detangle from Johnny to follow his grandfather's drumbeat.

"Then don't," Johnny said, and they seemed to twist closer.

John faded from their sight, but the drumbeat continued on. They turned toward it together, and just by focusing on it, moved nearer, until they were once again in the room where their bodies were.

"Hurry up!" Horace said, yelling down through that stairway hidden beneath the desk. "We need the oils to bind their souls to the bodies! What's taking so long?"

Two hooded figures came up the stairs, each holding a glass vial with liquid inside, and Maya knew without a doubt there was not oil in either of those vials. They held sea water, water from the storm mixed with water from the ocean, nothing that could harm her.

"At last!" Julie said. And then she injected Kevin, who lay beside her on the floor. And then she took up another hypodermic and injected herself herself. She clutched her chest, exhaled, and closed her eyes.

"Hurry, draw the sigils on the bodies!" Horace cried. "And then it will be our turn!"

The two hooded figures nodded, but one of them paused to push the desk back over the opening in the floor before moving closer. It moved easily. One of the new arrivals knelt beside Maya's body, the other beside Johnny's.

As that dark hood leaned closer, and Maya felt her and knew her. The person wearing the monk's robe was Kiley. Not Tilda, not Beasley, but Kiley. And the one who knelt near Johnny was Breia. She didn't know what had happened down below, but somehow Kiley and Breia must have ambushed the cultists and taken their robes.

Kiley leaned low and pulled the talisman off Maya's neck. Maya knew the talisman was supposed to guide Julie's soul into her own body. But Kiley removed it, then spun fast, and draped it over Julie's neck instead. "Keep your nasty ass soul in your own body," she whispered.

Breia, who swam in her monk's robe, did the same with Johnny, taking off the talisman and returning to Kevin's neck.

Then suddenly, Breia dropped to the floor with a soft gasp, and emerged from her own fallen body in death fairy form. And she looked fierce. Her eyes had gone black, and her wings were no longer fluffy and white, but sharp and vivid red. And nobody in the room seemed able to see her.

"Breia!" Maya cried, overjoyed to see her friend again, and seeing her in a far different way than she ever had before. She could see her soul, her mighty, powerful soul. She was far more than any of them had known.

Below them, Kiley was locked in combat with Horace, who'd caught on and grabbed her.

"Maya, Johnny! You have to get back into your bodies," Breia said.

Maya said, "I don't think we can. They aren't alive anymore."

"Grandfather said to follow the drumbeat, but I can no longer hear it," Johnny added.

Breia looked down, then she vanished. A second later, she was back in her body, getting up from the floor, whipping off the stupid hooded cloak, and racing for cube table. She grabbed two syringes marked with green labels while Horace and Kiley were locked in combat.

Horace landed a blow to Kiley's head, knocking her to the floor, and then he turned and went after Breia.

Instinctively, Maya threw up her hands, and when she did, her body on the floor did, too. Its arms rose up, palms flat, and a blast of power hit Horace so hard he sailed backward and smashed straight through a window, the only one that was no longer shuttered. His scream as he fell three stories was swallowed up by the storm's furious howl.

Kiley turned to gape at Maya's body on the floor.

I can't see what's happening, dammit! Lady El said, and Maya was stunned that she could hear her.

Kiley wrestled out of her robe. Breia knelt down to inject Johnny with the green-labeled drug, the one that was supposed to restart his heart. Then she did the same to Maya.

Then she and Kiley sat on the floor, staring at their bodies, waiting, talking to them. "Come on, come back, come back to us. We need you guys. Come on." Kiley was shaking Jack, smacking his cheeks to bring him around, even untying his hands from behind him, but she never took her eyes from the bodies of her friends. Breia had already untied Joe and was shaking his shoulder with one hand, equally riveted. "Come on," she whispered. "Please, please, please,"

John Redhawk's drumbeat started up again. Maya heard it, distant and faint, but growing steadily louder. *Ba-bum, ba-bum, ba-bum.*

"I hear it," Johnny said. "Do you hear it, Maya? Grandfather's drum."

"I hear it," she said. "But it's two drums beating as one. Our heartbeats, I think."

He gazed into her very being. "I don't want to let you go."

"Maybe you don't have to," she said. Their gazes held for a moment, then they turned their attention to their bodies on the floor, and she said, "I feel so wide and deep and high. How are we ever going to fit back in those tiny things?"

And then there was a sensation of falling, and she startled awake just like when you fall in a dream as she landed back in her body. She sucked in a loud, rasping breath that filled her lungs to bursting, then exhaled it fully as Breia cheered and Kiley crawled over to her and hugged her, lifting her body up to do so.

Jack was sitting up and rubbing his head. Joe was still lying down, but he moaned, blinking his eyes. They'd been nearest the white smoke, had breathed in more of it than the others had.

Maya pushed past the embraces of her friends, and crawled on hands and knees to Johnny. "Come back," she said. "Follow the drumbeat of our hearts." She laid her head on his chest, and it was silent. "Follow the drumbeat of mine, then," she said, and she laid across his chest, so her heart was directly atop his.

She felt it when it beat again. She felt the sudden, powerful thud beneath her, and the rhythm came next. *Ba-bum, ba-bum.* He dragged in an open-mouthed breath, and his arms snapped around her.

She turned so she could see his face as his eyes opened. He gazed into hers, gazed more deeply than anyone ever had, saw more of her than anyone ever could, and then he lifted his head and he kissed her. Her arms slid beneath him and she kissed him back.

KILEY GOT Jack into an upright position, rubbing his back as he coughed. His eyes were red, and she was mad as hell at the assholes who'd gassed him. When his head cleared enough, Jack watched Johnny and Maya making out for a second, blinking in confusion.

"What the heck did I miss?"

"My theory is that something happened between them while they were dead," Kiley said.

Lady El said, *I'm going to file a complaint. My death had no such perks!*

"Are you okay?" Jack asked. "Did they hurt you?"

"I hurt them, actually. The two whose robes we borrowed anyway. We left them down in the cave. Bashed 'em in the head, then tied them up with their own sashes. But they're alive." Then she glanced at Breia. "They're still alive, right? We didn't bash them too hard with our rocks, did we?"

"I'm not feeling the pull."

Hearing their conversation, Maya and Johnny stopped kissing and sat up, but kept their arms around each other and their bodies pressed close.

"I controlled it, Johnny," Breia said, her voice light with excitement. "When you left your bodies, I felt the pull, but Kiley told me to take charge, to refuse to leave until I was ready, and I *did it*. Well, for a few minutes, anyway. And when I did emerge, I stayed invisible. You know, to the living."

"I'm so proud of you, Bray," he said.

Maya beamed at her but didn't speak. Her eyes brimmed with tears but they didn't spill over.

"What about the rest of them?" Kiley asked. She gazed at the two bodies on the floor, the broken and twisted, and very, very dead Kevin, and Julie, young and flawless and beautiful. "Jack, are they still here? Do you see their spirits?" Kiley asked. "Breia, do you feel them?"

"I don't feel them," Breia said. "Either they're still alive or they died and crossed over without any problem."

"The barrier wouldn't let them do that, though. Would it?."

There was a sound, a roaring, sloshing sound from below. Maya followed the noise to the cube desk and pushed it aside, and then her hand flew to her lips and she whispered, "Oh no!"

Kiley ran to her side and leaned over. Water had filled the cave below and had come halfway up the stone staircase.

"The storm surge must've washed the stones and wards away. It demolished the barrier from below," Maya said softly.

"The souls that were trapped here crossed to the other side freely," Breia said. She closed her eyes. "They're gone, all of them. Arthur. Kevin. Horace died from his fall out the window. Tilda and Beasley ...they must've drowned." She closed her eyes and bowed her head. "Without the barrier to hold them here, their souls crossed the veil in the blink of any eye. They closed their eyes here, and opened them there. And that's the way it's supposed to work. I only get involved if they feel stuck or can't find their way."

"I don't understand," Maya said. "If the barrier was down then why didn't Johnny and I cross over?"

"I don't know," Breia looked around. "Why ask me? I just figured out how to go invisible yesterday."

"It wasn't our time." Johnny said it aloud, and Kiley heard Lady El say it at the same time, and nodded her agreement.

"We still have things to do here, I guess." Maya leaned closer to him, and their arms were still locked around each other's waists.

Julie moaned and stirred. Everyone took a big giant step away from her as she sat up, holding her head. "What a rush," she said, and then she looked at her hand, then at her clothing. "No. No! What happened? Arthur? Arthur!"

"Arthur and Kevin have moved on," Kiley said. "And Horace and Beasley and Tilda too. As for you, I guess you get to spend what's left of your time on earth behind bars. Karma's such a bitch, isn't she?"

Julie folded over herself and wept as Kiley went behind her to bind her hands behind her back.

"Let's make our way to that boathouse and the radios," Jack said. "We'll get some help out here as soon as the storm has cleared."

He led the way down the metal staircase, pushing Julie ahead of him. Everyone followed him through Arthur's former suite, where he let go of Julie. "You can wait the storm out here," he said. "The worst has passed, the water won't come up this high." He tied the rope around the metal stairway's railing.

"Don't ...you can't leave me here."

"Don't worry, Julie," Kiley said. "The storm's abating, like he said. And we've taken care of your ghost problem for you. You've got nothing to fear here. Nothing at all, except your own dark soul."

They left her there, sobbing, and headed down the hall to the broad split staircase. Jack and Joe ran across to the east wing, and returned with everyone's bags, which had already been mostly packed and waiting. Then they continued down to the ground floor.

"What's in the pillowcase, Maya?" Kiley asked, noticing that Maya carried it bunched up in one hand, with its bottom dangling and obviously heavy.

"I took Arthur and Julie's. I didn't want to touch them with my hands, so, makeshift sack," she said, holding it up.

"What will you do with them?" Kiley asked.

"Toss them into the sea as an offering to the dark goddesses who answered my call tonight and set things right."

"The boathouse is a short walk," Joe said. "And the storm is passing quickly."

Jack nodded, and they all headed outside. The rain was still falling as they walked the winding path down the cliffs. Jack held Kiley's hand. Joe kept an arm around Breia, who didn't seem as exhausted as she had the last time she'd popped out of her body. She seemed energized, in fact. And as for Maya and Johnny, they were so locked at the hip it was like they'd melded or something.

As they made it to the beach and followed it toward the boat house, Kiley saw that one of the boats had escaped captivity, and bobbed peacefully on the shore.

"This is a perfect plan, Joe," Jack said, and they all turned to head toward that boat. "You've been a tremendous help through all this. You ever think of changing jobs?"

"And giving up the luxurious life of being a science teacher in a public school where half the parents and a handful of staff remain unconvinced the earth is round? Not on your life." Then he glanced at Breia and said, "But I do have summers off, and in a pinch, I can get a sub." He winked at her, and she beamed.

Jack pulled Kiley closer to his side as they walked behind the others. Joe and Breia were in front, with Johnny and Maya right behind them. Softly he said, "I'm sorry about all this."

Kiley grinned at him. "I'm *jealous* about all this."

"Of Julie? Still?" he asked, looking stunned.

"Of those two." She nodded ahead of them toward Maya and Johnny. You could not fit a toothpick in between them. "I missed you, when we were at odds," she said. "I hated being mad at you."

"I hated you being mad at me, too." He pulled her closer, his arm around her waist until they walked touching from shoulder to knee.

"Something happened between those two," Kiley said. "While they were out of their bodies, I think. Can you imagine?"

"I wonder if Johnny will ever tell me what." Jack glanced his friend's way but quickly returned his eyes to Kiley's.

"Maya will tell me," Kiley said, "eventually. But in the meantime, I have to tell you, I think all this might've made me love you even more than I already did."

He stopped walking. Joe and the others had reached the small boat, and waded into the surf to grab its tow lines and pull it toward the pier. The wind still blew, but it was no longer raining. And in the distance, black clouds parted to reveal a jigsaw puzzle piece of the sun rising in the east. Its light spread, seeming to push the storm even further away, and its golden glow spilled onto the sea, to calm and soothe its roiling waves.

"I'm very glad to hear that," Jack said, "It'll make for an even more special wedding."

"Wed—*what*?" Kiley stopped walking and backed two steps away from him, gaping, eyes wide. "Was that a proposal?"

"No," Jack said. "This is." He pulled a box from his pocket. "I've been carrying this around since we left the mainland. Thought paradise would be the perfect place to ask, but now here we are, in the aftermath of a tropical storm, or maybe a cat one, at the break of dawn, with a trail of baddies and bodies in our wake. Not the perfect setting for a proposal. But at least there are palm trees, and sand, and an ocean, even if it does seem angry at the moment. So I'm asking. Marry me, Kiley. Let's make this partnership of ours official."

Kiley gazed down at him, her heart filled to overflowing. She was aware of her beloved friends, who'd all stopped what they were doing and turned to watch them. Maya was holding steepled hands in front of her mouth, and Breia was bouncing up and down and smiling ear to ear.

She gazed down at Jack, then looked around them. Waves

crashed against rocks. Palm fronds swayed in the ever less brutal winds and the rising sun revealed a debris-littered beach.

"This *is* the perfect setting for a proposal," she said, "for us, anyway."

"And?"

And? Lady El asked. *Don't torture the poor guy, say yes!*

"Yes," Kiley said.

Everyone cheered. Jack sprang upright, scooping her off her feet, twirling her in a circle, and then kissing her like there was no tomorrow.

JOHNNY DROVE THE SMALL BOAT, and Maya, who couldn't seem to bear not being in physical contact with him ever since they'd returned to their bodies, sat beside him. The seats were white vinyl, like the horseshoe of bench seats in the stern. It was a small boat, but there was room for the six of them.

She still had the pillowcase in her hand. When the shoreline was within sight, she looked at Johnny and nodded once. He eased back the throttle, until the small craft merely kept its course at a snail's pace.

Maya stood up and raised her arms upward in the shape of a crescent, holding the talismans by their chains.

Everyone fell into respectful silence.

"Mother of oceans, mother of the seas, cleanse the golden talismans I offer unto thee. Gold and silver baubles from the earth you came. I return you now for the goddess to reclaim. Mothers of the underworld who helped to set things right, take these offerings with thee into the night. So mote it be."

Her friends had been with her long enough by now to know to repeat those final four words. "So mote it be."

She smiled and nodded, then leaned over the side to rinse

her hands in the salty water.

Johnny pushed the throttle forward, and they resumed their trek back to shore. The others fell into quiet conversation behind them, but Johnny couldn't seem to stop turning his head to look into her eyes, and she couldn't take her eyes off him.

"So," he said at length. "Now that we've been dead together ..."

"Let's try being alive together," she said, finishing his thought. "I saw you, Johnny. I still see you."

"Me, too. Like I never have before."

It was hard for Maya to put into words the power of what she had felt for him when they'd been outside their bodies, their souls entwined, a double helix. There were no words. But she sensed that he'd felt exactly what she had.

"Your grandfather," she said, a small ripple of unease moving through her. "We saw him. Do you think that means ...?"

"He's alive. That mountain in the background, I've seen it before. He had a framed print of it in his living room. Denali."

"He's in Alaska?" she asked.

"He was at that moment, at least," he said. Then he looked at her and smiled again. His hand cupped her face, and he leaned in for a kiss. Then he said, "Man, this is something. You and me. This feeling. This is *really* something."

She leaned close and whispered close enough so that her breath would tickle his ear. "Feels a little like magic, to me."

He laughed softly, and she did, too. As she rested her head on his shoulder, somewhere beyond the whooshing waves and buzzing motor, she thought she heard the rhythmic beat of his grandfather's drum.

The End...
Not

ALSO BY MAGGIE SHAYNE

SMALLTOWN CONTEMPORARY & WESTERN ROMANCE

The Texas Brand Series

The Littlest Cowboy

The Baddest Virgin in Texas

Badlands Bad Boy

Long Gone Lonesome Blues

The Lone Cowboy

Lone Star Lonely

The Outlaw Bride

Texas Angel

Texas Homecoming

The Oklahoma Brands

The Brands Who Came for Christmas

Brand New Heartache

Secrets and Lies

A Mommy for Christmas

One Magic Summer

Sweet Vidalia Brand

The McIntyre Men

Oklahoma Christmas Blues

Oklahoma Moonshine

Oklahoma Starshine

Shine On, Oklahoma

Oklahoma Sunshine

<u>Shattered Sisters</u>

Reckless

Forgotten

Broken

Hollow

<u>Secrets of Shadow Falls</u>

Killing Me Softly

Kill Me Again

Kiss Me, Kill Me

PARANORMAL ROMANCE

<u>The Immortals (More planned)</u>

Eternity

Infinity

Destiny

Immortality

<u>By Magic</u>

By Magic Beguiled

By Magic Enchanted

By Magic Born

By Magic Granted

The Fatal Series (Ongoing)

Fatal Fixer Upper

Fatal But Festive

Fatal Family Secrets

NOVELLAS

Everything She Does is Magic

Spellbound

Magic by Moonlight

Witch Moon

Talk Doggy to Me

Ms. Terwilliger Goes Rogue

The Widow's Timeless Wager

Unmasked

Night Vision

Get Home Before Moonrise

Solstice

Zombies! A Love Story

Holly and the Humbug

STAND-ALONE NOVELS

Star Gazer

Miranda's Viking

ABOUT THE AUTHOR

New York Times and *USA Today* bestselling novelist Maggie Shayne has published sixty-two novels and twenty-two novellas for five major publishers over the course of twenty-two years. She also spent a year writing for American daytime TV dramas *The Guiding Light* and *As the World Turns* and was offered the position of co-head writer of the former; a million-dollar offer she tearfully turned down. It was scary, turning down an offer that big. But her heart was in her books, and she'd found it impossible to do both.

In March 2014, she did something even scarier. She left the world's largest publisher and went "indie."

Now, she is embarking on an exciting new leg of her publishing journey with most of her titles moving to small press publisher, Oliver Heber Books.

Maggie's *Wings in the Night* series and her non-fiction spiritual self-help books continue to be published through Maggie's own company, Thunderfoot Publishing.

Maggie writes smalltown contemporary romances like the recent *McIntyre Men* series, which boasts "a miracle in every story." She cut her teeth on western-themed category romances like her classics *The Texas Brand* and *The Oklahoma Brands*.

Later, Maggie expanded into romantic suspense and thrillers like *The Mordecai Young series, The Secrets of Shadow Falls*, and her career-best, *The Brown and de Luca Novels*.

She is perhaps best known for her beloved paranormal romances, perennial favorites *The Immortals*, the *By Magic series*, and one of the first vampire romance series ever published, (and still ongoing) *Wings in the Night*.

Now she's writing a series of page turning rom-com ghost mysteries, *The Fatal Series*.

Maggie is a fifteen-time RITA® Award nominee and one-time winner. She has received more than thirty other industry awards for her work, and has been nominated for many more.

She lives in the rolling green and forested hilltops of Cortland County NY, wine & dairy country, despite having sworn off both. She is a vegan Wiccan hippy living her best life with her beloved husband Lance, and usually at least two dogs.

Maggie also writes spiritual self-help books and runs an online magic shop, BlissBlog.org

For additional information, visit Maggie's website.
www.maggieshayne.com

Email Maggie @ maggie@maggieshayne.com